So much for h[illegible] pooh-poohed [illegible] being a man c[illegible] thought weakly.

He was tall, with a lithe, broad-shouldered, lean-hipped body that was in perfect proportion to his height. His hair was dark, not black, but a deep, dark mahogany that the sun had streaked here and there with attractive splashes of coppery gold.

'Are you lost?'

'No,' he said, one delicately arched eyebrow rising quizzically. 'Why—are you?'

'No, of course I'm not,' exclaimed Ginny, only too aware of the flustered picture she was presenting.

'I. . . Who are you?'

'Michael Grant,' he replied, a faint hint of amusement in the vivid blue eyes. 'And I can only assume that you are one of Libby's many and varied friends.'

Kate Proctor is part Irish and part Welsh, though she spent most of her childhood in England and several years of her adult life in Central Africa. Now divorced, she lives just outside London with her two cats, Florence and Minnie, presented to her by her two daughters who live fairly close by. Having given up her career as a teacher on her return to England, Kate now devotes most of her time to writing. Her hobbies include crossword puzzles, bridge and, at the moment, learning Spanish.

Recent titles by the same author:

A PASSIONATE DECEIT

TALL, DARK AND DANGEROUS

BY

KATE PROCTOR

MILLS & BOON

Harlequin Mills & Boon Limited,
Eton House, 18–24 Paradise Road, Richmond, Surrey TW9 1SR
This edition published by arrangement with
Harlequin Enterprises B.V.

ISBN 0 263 79247 1

Set in 10 on 11½ pt Linotron Times
01-9510-53418

Typeset in Great Britain by CentraCet, Cambridge
Made and printed in Great Britain

CHAPTER ONE

GINNY PRICE flopped down on the cobbled terrace, a sigh of frustration escaping her as she leaned back against the huge, plant-filled terracotta pot with which she had been wrestling. It had been heavy enough empty, she reflected exasperatedly, and now it weighed a ton. Only a complete idiot would have filled the wretched thing before positioning it in its destined spot—and she was that idiot!

But at least she had finished the Lebauts' garden without committing any similar amateurish blunder, she consoled herself, and even better, she had been generously paid for her efforts. Her spirit boosted by the memory, she lazily brushed some of the soil from her cut-down denim dungarees before adjusting her battered straw hat, almost the same colour as the short-cropped hair capping her head, and let the late afternoon Mediterranean sun play against the tanned oval of her face.

With Libby's baby due in two months, it was wise to get all the money they could in the kitty, she thought, a dreamy smile widening the generous curve of her mouth, just to be sure they had every possible contingency covered.

For one who had never in her life had to take the cost of anything into consideration, Libby had become a zealous convert to economising, thought Ginny with a lazy chuckle of indulgence.

'It's not as though I'll not be seeing someone just as qualified as Sylvie,' Libby had stated, with the studied firmness of one not wholly convinced, having learned, during her last check-up in Cannes that her obstetrician, a woman who had gone to endless lengths to gain her confidence, would be spending the following month at a sister clinic in Paris. 'I mean, she did say I could see her in Paris, if I wanted. . .'

'And you obviously want,' Ginny had laughed, giving the plainly troubled American girl a comforting hug. She knew that an emergency appendectomy at an early age had left Libby decidedly edgy about matters medical—and how ruthlessly her friend had suppressed all her fears for the sake of the baby she was carrying. 'So go ahead. That friend of yours, Jeanne, has invited you to stay with her often enough—and she knows about the baby. . .'

Ginny sat up, frowning, her thoughts scattered by the sight of a car turning up the drive. It was a white, open-topped sports car, one of those fortunes on wheels, she noted with amusement, that Libby would probably have been able to identify in an instant.

She craned her neck as the car, instead of stopping and reversing as she had expected, continued up the drive towards her. The driver probably realised it was semi-circular and would keep going, she told herself, only to find the car drawing to a halt beside her.

It was as the man stepped from the car, and while Ginny was scrambling inelegantly to her feet, that she got her first real sight of him and found herself having to bite back an exclamation of disbelief. So much for her always having pooh-poohed the idea of there being a man of her dreams, she thought weakly—though this particular man, appearing as if from the blue, was no doubt the physical embodiment of a good many women's dreams!

He was tall, perhaps an inch or two over six feet,

with a lithe, broad-shouldered, lean-hipped body that was in perfect proportion to his height. His hair was dark, not the black her first glimpse had taken it to be, but a deep, dark mahogany that the sun had streaked here and there with attractive splashes of coppery gold. With all this man had going for him, thought Ginny with amused disbelief, he could afford a flaw or two where his features were concerned. But apart from the decidedly bad-tempered expression adorning the chiselled perfection of those features she was now minutely examining, there was nothing she found that could be remotely described as a flaw. And as for the dark luxuriance of the lashes surrounding those wide-spaced, startlingly blue eyes, she thought with amused fascination that she could think of a number of women who would kill to possess them!

It was only when the man stopped speaking and flung her a look of undisguised impatience that the fact hit Ginny that he had been speaking—in French far too rapid for her grasp, and in an accent very much like Libby's.

Dear God, the man was American, she thought, her intrigued amusement flattened by a sudden rush of panic.

'It's all right. . . I mean, I do speak English,' she cut in disjointedly, when the man again began addressing her in French. 'In fact, I am English,' she waffled inanely. 'Are you lost?'

It was a question inspired by naïve wishfulness and one, a sudden flash of intuitive pessimism warned her, with as much hope of receiving an affirmative answer as she had of flying to the moon.

'No,' he said, one delicately arched brow rising quizzically. 'Why—are you?'

'No, of course I'm not,' exclaimed Ginny, only too

aware of the flustered picture she was presenting. 'It's just that we don't often come across strangers around here,' she added half-heartedly.

'That's the whole idea of having a place like this,' he murmured in that attractively drawly accent so like Libby's. 'You don't often get pestered by trespassing strangers. . . So, tell me, who are you?'

'I'm the gardener,' stammered Ginny, too thrown by the question either to notice its innuendo or to query his right to be asking it. 'The person who owns the place isn't here at the moment.'

'On the contrary,' he said, giving her an unsettlingly ambivalent look before turning and lifting a couple of gleaming leather cases from the back of the car, 'the person who owns it is right here before you.'

'I. . . Who are you?' croaked Ginny, her knees threatening to buckle beneath her—Libby had sworn her family always gave the company overseeing the estate at least a couple of weeks' notice before arriving!

'Michael Grant,' he replied, a faint hint of amusement in the vivid blue of the eyes taking open stock of her obvious consternation. 'And I can only assume you're one of Libby's many and varied friends,' he added. For an instant, Ginny thought he was about to hold out a hand for her to shake; it rose, instead, to clutch theatrically at his head. 'Sorry—I forgot—you're the gardener.'

'I'm also a friend of Libby's,' stated Ginny, acutely aware of the distaste behind his reference to Libby's 'many and varied friends'. He could hardly be expected to know that she held similar feelings towards that group of ruthless spongers who had once peopled Libby's life, but who were now, mercifully, no longer part of it.

'OK, so you're a friend of Libby's,' he stated without interest, picking up his luggage and striding towards the creeper-clad villa. 'I've driven straight through from Paris, so you'll forgive me if my only interest is in getting into a bath-tub and sluicing off the grime from the journey rather than socialising with you right now.'

Had she just driven five hundred miles or so, mused Ginny as she followed him into the house, she would have resembled a limp rag; yet there was barely a crease in the pale, immaculately tailored lightweight trousers of the man striding nonchalantly ahead of her, nor even in the dark silk shirt skimming with no trace of dampness the broad contours of his back.

She halted momentarily in her tracks, her exasperated intake of breath audible as she realised that it was the appalling problem of Michael Grant's presence she should be dwelling on rather than his undeniable sartorial elegance.

'Did you say something?' he demanded, a look of irritation on his handsome features as he turned his head to her.

'No,' muttured Ginny, feeling hopelessly out of her depth. 'But I was about to make tea—would you like some. . .or coffee, perhaps?'

'Now, that's original—the gardener offering me tea in my own place,' he murmured, the scowl darkening. 'Don't tell me you're a live-in gardener?'

'But I am,' protested Ginny, colour rushing mortifyingly to her cheeks. 'I mean. . . I do. . .live here, that is. I do the housekeeping as well as the gardening.'

'You don't say,' he drawled, his eyes narrowing in undisguised scrutiny. 'And my niece—is she around?'

His niece, thought Ginny weakly, her mind scrabbling in vain to dredge up what it could on Libby's tyrannical family. He could only be around thirty—surely too young to be an uncle?

'She's in Paris. . .she went to see some friends.'

'I'm surprised she didn't move them all down here with her,' he stated, sarcasm oozing from his every word. 'Or are you about to tell me she's filled the place and is off visiting with the overspill?'

'Only the two of us are staying here,' replied Ginny, stung by the undisguised hostility of his tone, but feeling a reluctant understanding in the light of Libby's chequered past. 'And, to put your mind at rest, Libby no longer mixes with the sort of people she once did.'

'So, you think my mind needs putting at rest, do you?' He hesitated, frowning. 'I don't know your name.'

'It's Ginny—Ginny Price.'

'And you're telling me you're not one of the usual free-loaders Libby has around her, is that it, Ginny?'

'I most certainly am not a free-loader!' she exclaimed with fiery indignation—now he was being downright rude.

'Glad to hear it,' he drawled, turning and continuing on into the house. 'I'll have the bedroom overlooking the cypress grove—if no one else is using it, that is.'

'No one's using it,' snapped Ginny. 'I'll see to bed-linen for you. If you'd let us know you were coming, I could have had everything ready for you.' As would any housekeeper-cum-gardener being paid the relative fortune she allegedly was, added Ginny silently to herself, her blood running cold at the mere thought.

'I'm the kind of guy who prefers doing things on the spur of the moment,' he retorted as be began climbing the wide, curving staircase. 'Give me half an hour or so to get myself cleaned up,' he added as he disappeared from view, 'then I'll gladly join you for tea.'

Ginny flew to the large, old-fashioned kitchen and flung herself down on one of the chairs at the huge, scrubbed wood table dominating it.

She had to get a grip on herself, think things through!

'Libby, what have you got me into?' she groaned softly, folding her arms against the table and lowering her head defeatedly on to them.

To most observers, the friendship that had sprung up between the rebellious American girl with a background of untold wealth, and the unnaturally subdued English girl without a penny to her name must have seemed one of the most unlikely imaginable.

'The reason we're over here is that my new stepmother is English—so my dad's doing research at Trinity,' the twelve-year-old Libby Collier had announced by way of introduction, on their first day at the small Cambridge secondary school at which Ginny would remain for the next four years and Libby for less than one.

'Will you still be my friend when I've gone?' Libby had later demanded, when their unlikely friendship had blossomed to a peculiarly mutual dependency.

'Why would you go?' Ginny had asked, devastated by even the thought of losing the one friend she had found in the barren new existence fate had imposed on her.

'I know I won't be here long,' Libby had stated with prophetic despondency. 'Jane's my third stepmother, but she won't last any longer than the others. In the academic world, my dad's considered some sort of genius, but he's just a birdbrain when it comes to personal relationships. He keeps saying my mom's the only woman he's ever truly loved. . . Why did she have to die?' she had railed disconsolately.

'At least you have your father!' Ginny had rounded on her friend with a savagery born of her own still-gaping wounds. 'Less than two years ago both my parents were killed in a car crash. That's why I had to come here. . .and live with an aunt who hates me!'

She gave a weary shake of her head as she lifted it from her arms. It wasn't strictly true to say that her aunt Irene hated her, she told herself bitterly, but there was no denying that the love her parents had lavished on her until the day they had been so brutally snatched from her ten-year-old life had had to last her the rest of her childhood.

Love had always been a stranger in Irene Bond's house. She had felt nothing but disapproval for the vivacious sister, fifteen years her junior, who had so often in her short life tried to wean her from the almost fanatically rigid set of her ways and from the gratuitous penny-pinching that coloured her every move. Irene had regarded the entry of that sister's child into her ordered life as nothing more than a chore to be tackled with the minimum of disruption to her routine.

Ginny gave another shake of her head, this time in an effort to rid it of the cloying bitterness of those memories.

Chalk and cheese she and Libby might have been, she reminisced sadly, but the mutual desperation of need that had first drawn them together had forged a bond between them that the years apart had never weakened.

She nearly jumped out of her skin at the sudden sound of the telephone ringing, then leapt to her feet and raced to the wall extension.

'Hi, Ginny! Bad news for the kitty, I'm afraid—I'm being kept in overnight at the clinic. Though it won't cost any more here than it does in Cannes and I'd have had to stay——'

'Libby, for heaven's sake, what's wrong?'

'My darned blood-sugar's up a bit again, but it's nothing to worry about—it's not even up as much as it was last time, but they're insisting on running all those tests again, but only to be one hundred and ten per cent on the safe side.'

'Poor you,' sympathised Ginny, silently thanking her lucky stars Libby had followed her obstetrician to Paris—there was no guaranteeing how she might have responded to that sort of news from another specialist. 'And don't you dare worry about the kitty—it's extremely healthy, thanks to the fact that the Lebauts have just paid me for the work I did on their garden. . . Libby, are you sure you're OK?'

'Ginny, I'm a pampered heiress,' teased Libby, sounding on top of the world, 'the sort who gets hospitalised for a month with an ingrown toe-nail—so stop fussing!'

'I'm not,' sighed Ginny. 'I just had to make sure you were up to hearing the news. . . Your uncle's just arrived.'

'David?' groaned Libby.

'He says his name's Michael,' said Ginny, her eyes widening with alarm. She knew relatively little about Libby's family, except that they were ghastly—and it hadn't even occurred to her to ask for proof of the caller's identity. 'He seems terribly young to be your uncle,' she added nervously.

'If the guy you're referring to looks as though he's just stepped off the cover of a movie magazine, that's my uncle Michael,' replied Libby hollowly. 'He's only about eight or nine years older than I am—the baby of the Grant dynasty, but lethal all the same.'

'He says he owns the villa.'

'Now you mention it, he does,' muttered Libby vaguely, her mind plainly on other things. 'Darn it, this is the last thing we need. . . Did he say how long he'd be staying?'

'No, but he obviously wasn't in the least pleased to find me in residence,' replied Ginny, then related what had happened.

'I should have realised one of them would show up here sooner or later to check on me,' stated Libby morosely. 'I guess Michael must be in France on business, but don't worry, he won't waste too much time hanging around waiting for me to show up—hotshot tycoons like him measure their time in bucks,' she added, equally morosely. 'Where is he right now?'

'Having a bath. Libby, what am I supposed to say to him?'

'Anything, as long as it's not the fact I'm pregnant—that's the last thing I need them knowing!'

'Not to mention the father-to-be,' exclaimed Ginny wearily, wondering, as she had innumerable times before, how her brash, rash friend always managed to end up in a muddle, even now, when she had matured beyond all recognition and had her life mapped out before her with the man she so passionately loved. 'Libby, you keep saying you intend making your peace with the Grants once you and Jean-Claude are married, but now that your uncle's here——'

'No! Now's completely the wrong time!'

'Libby, don't you think it's time you sat down and had a serious rethink about all this—at least about contacting Jean-Claude and telling him about the baby?'

'We've been through all that,' protested Libby

edgily. 'Ginny, don't even *think* about telling Michael anything. I just couldn't handle it right now.'

'Libby, love, I shan't tell him a thing,' exclaimed Ginny. 'You know I wouldn't—but just what am I supposed to say to him?'

'Just stall him!' the American girl begged, a note of panic entering her tone. 'Tell him I'm in Paris on business—you never know, he might even swallow it, once he's finished laughing. . . I don't know,' she sighed, sounding suddenly very unsure of herself. 'Just tell him you don't know when I'll be back.'

'Don't worry—I'll come up with something,' said Ginny, that uncharacteristic note of vulnerability in Libby's voice making her inject a confidence she was far from feeling into her words. 'You're not to worry.'

'I can't help it with Michael around—I'm just not up to facing the Grants yet,' sighed Libby, then unexpectedly gave one of her irrepressible chuckles. 'You know, if I didn't know you so well, I'd say Michael would be a great choice for you to loosen up with and get rid of those sexual hang-ups you claim you don't have.'

'Libby!'

'Don't worry, I'm not recommending it,' laughed Libby. 'He's far too dangerous for you—you'd probably end up in love with him.'

'So, the man actually has a few lovable points,' teased Ginny, relieved to hear Libby's laughter, despite its cause.

'Oh, he's lovable, all right,' sighed Libby. 'And I was one of his greatest fans until a while back—not that I ever saw as much of him as I'd have liked. Being so much nearer my age, he never went in for breathing down my neck the way the rest of the family did. . .or so I kidded myself. It was Michael's spying on me and reporting back to Grandpa and David that resulted in my not getting control of my own money once I reached twenty-one.'

Ginny felt a twinge of guilt as she found herself thinking that Libby, at twenty-one, was the last person to whom anyone in his right mind would have handed over control of a considerable fortune.

'Ginny, I know what you're thinking,' said Libby, 'and you're right, but it was the low-down way he went about it that blew him as far as I was concerned. Even in my wildest days, I always had a few decent friends—and not all of them stuck away on the other side of the Atlantic. Michael picked one as his victim and seduced her into telling him all she knew about me—then he dropped her like a hot potato.'

'Charming!' exclaimed Ginny, wrinkling her nose in disgust. 'Luckily I'm far too sexually repressed for that sort of ploy to work on me,' she added teasingly, while inwardly squirming at the memory of her initial reaction to him—there had been nothing in the least repressed about that. 'Anyway, we're probably making far too much of this—for all we know, this is just a flying visit.'

'You're right,' agreed Libby. 'Luckily Jeanne has said it's OK for me to stay at her place as long as I like. See if you can find out how long he reckons on being around—I'll give you a call tomorrow.'

'What if he answers the phone?'

'So I'll speak to him—and tell him how sorry I am to have missed him. Meanwhile, watch yourself—the way that guy wields charm, repression doesn't get a look-in!'

Charm? What charm? During the past few hours the man had displayed about as much charm as a rattlesnake, Ginny fumed to herself, as she carried a tray of coffee out on to the terrace after dinner.

It was one of those evenings of balmy perfection, the sort that, no matter how many times she experienced it, she knew she would never grow to take for granted. Sitting on the terrace, listening to the innumerable sounds that filled the silence of the night as they drank their coffee, was a ritual she and Libby had fallen into of late. But tonight there was an oppressive charge in the air that had nothing to do with the weather and everything to do with the man now taking a seat beside her.

He was so impossibly good-looking, she thought with a twinge of exasperation, so much so that she kept finding herself watching him with slightly detached disbelief instead of preparing herself for the moment when he would pounce. And pounce he most certainly would, she warned herself nervously, because, apart from the anger that had briefly flashed across his features when she had first told him, he had taken the news of Libby's phone call, and the lack of any mention of her return, with barely a comment. But over dinner his cloak of restrained urbanity had begun slipping, to an extent that he had begun reminding her of her aunt Irene in the manner he had of looking down his decidedly patrician nose at her as he delivered his carefully chosen barbs.

'Let's see if I have this right,' he murmured ominously, as they drank their coffee. 'You're my gardener,' he stated, giving slight, but none the less calculated emphasis to the possessive pronoun.

Ginny felt her heart plummet as she wondered if he was aware that he was paying the top rate for both a gardener and a housekeeper.

'And you also keep house for me,' he continued.

Ginny remained silent, battling against rising to the deliberate edge of offensiveness in his tone as she waited for her worst fears to be confirmed.

'But then, I've been paying you pretty well for both these jobs,' he murmured silkily. 'I don't have any beef about the housekeeping—your excellent cooking's worth every cent of that. It's the keeping up the grounds——'

'Keeping up the grounds?' exploded Ginny as she lost the battle with herself. 'Either your memory doesn't serve you in the least well, Mr Grant, or you know nothing about gardens. This place was a wilderness when I took it on! Nobody had touched the place since your last gardener retired.'

'He'd only been gone a couple of months when you started,' he retorted. 'Hardly enough time for the place to deteriorate into the wilderness you're claiming it was.'

Ginny took a gulp of her drink, simply to prevent herself retaliating. If what he said was true, the garden had been neglected for several months before her predecessor had retired, not that she saw anything to be gained by pointing that out to him.

'And, even though I am technically your employer, you don't have to call me Mr Grant—Michael will do.'

'And you may call me Ginny,' she retorted, incensed by his patronising tone.

'I hadn't intended calling you anything else,' he informed her with a hint of a chuckle. 'Tell me, Ginny, what brought you to France?'

'Several things, really,' she parried, unsettled by the sheer unexpectedness of the question and the mish-mash of unpleasant memories it evoked. 'I felt like a change of scenery.' And that, she supposed grimly, was one way of putting it; except that with a married boss who couldn't keep his hands to himself and an aunt who had literally shown her the door once her problems at work had become the subject of speculative gossip, a change of scenery had become a vital necessity. Libby's coinciding cry for help had been one she had responded to by cashing in her savings and taking off for France without a moment's hesitation.

'What—you decided you'd like to try gardening here instead of back home in England?'

'No, I. . . Yes.' She broke off, furious with herself for having become so visibly flustered. 'I wasn't doing gardening in England. . .but it's what I've always wanted to do.' It would have been safer to lie, she thought exasperatedly, and it would have given her a bit of practice for all the lies she would have to start coming up with in the very near future.

'So, you decided you'd cut your teeth on my property, did you?' he enquired with chilling softness.

'Of course I didn't,' she exclaimed, reliving all the misgivings she had felt when Libby had airily informed her that, apart from billing the villa accounts for the services of a housekeeper to augment their income, they would also claim for a gardener. 'I did an introductory gardening and landscaping course——'

'Introductory?'

'I had hoped to go on to do the full course, but wasn't able to.' And probably never would, since her savings towards that course had been what she and Libby had lived on at first. 'But I haven't had any complaints about my work yet—unless, that is, you intend making one now.'

'If I find anything to complain about, you'll hear me loud and clear,' he replied, draining his cup and rising.

Ginny watched in mounting disbelief as his tall figure

strode to the terrace steps—surely he didn't intend checking out her work here and now—in the dark!

'I'd almost forgotten what made me fall in love with this place,' he announced as he gazed around him.

Ginny gave a start of surprise, remembering how she too had fallen in love at her first sight of the villa, and her inability to accept the idea of such a place not being lived in to the hilt, but instead being merely one of several rarely used retreats owned by a family to whom money was plainly not a consideration.

'One of the reasons I decided to come here was to see for myself what sort of shape the place is in and what, if anything, needs doing to it,' he said as he returned to the table.

'But it's perfect,' protested Ginny before she could bite back the words.

'Even perfection starts fraying at the edges if it's not properly maintained,' he mocked, pouring them both more coffee—the first time he had lifted so much as a finger since his arrival, Ginny noted caustically. 'And those agents of mine don't exactly break their backs earning their fees.' He sat down. 'So, tell me about yourself, Ginny,' he said conversationally. 'I'm interested in your connection with my niece.'

'We went to school together in England,' she replied, striving to remain calm in the face of his aptitude for making even the most harmless of statements sound faintly derogatory.

'Oh, the English stepmother—she didn't last any longer than the rest of them,' he muttered almost to himself. 'Libby could only have been a kid then.'

'We were both twelve.'

'That must be one hell of a friendship the two of you struck up, to have survived that long,' he observed sceptically. 'She couldn't have been in England more than five minutes.'

'We were at school together for almost a year,' corrected Ginny, trying in vain to mask her growing resentment. 'And not only did we write to one another, we also managed to meet once or twice over the years. Of all her ex-stepmothers, Jane's the one Libby is closest to and still sees whenever she can.'

'From what I've heard, it was always handy for Libby to have England to escape to from whatever mess she got herself into in the States,' he stated, his heavy-lidded eyes coolly watchful. 'Though it seems she's now traded in England for France. . . Or will she end up running back to England from here this time, instead of from the States?'

'I suppose it's never occurred to you that it might be her family she's always running from?' exploded Ginny, and instantly regretted her outburst. 'Look, I'm sorry—I had no right to say that,' she apologised, certain she had, but even more certain that if she didn't get her temper in hand she would end up giving something away.

'No, you hadn't,' he agreed, his eyes blazing. 'So Libby's still running, is she? If that's the case, I think it's time we cut the pussy-footing and got on to what it is you and she are up to here!'

'Up to?' croaked Ginny. 'We're not up to anything! And you misunderstood me—I didn't mean to imply Libby was actually running from you now!'

'So what's she doing?'

'How do you mean, exactly?'

He flashed her a look of irritation. 'A couple of years back, Libby got herself involved with a playboy French aristocrat—a guy with about as much idea of responsibility as she has—and later followed him to

France. He disappeared off the scene several months ago and she's been living down here ever since—and no one's heard a word from her.'

'*I've* heard from her!' retorted Ginny, astounded by how much he seemed to know. But if only he knew the rest of it; how, accepting they both had irresponsible pasts to live down, Jean-Claude and Libby had agreed to his parents' conditions to giving their marriage their blessing—a year's total separation, during which time Jean-Claude proved himself in the family business and neither came within a hair's breadth of scandal. 'I've heard from her,' repeated Ginny, the words losing their edge of indignation as she struggled to shake free from those thoughts. 'She wrote and asked me to join her here.'

'That's not the story you were giving me a few moments ago.'

'I wasn't giving you a *story* a few moments ago,' she protested, his tone re-igniting her indignation. 'My wanting a change of scenery happened to coincide with Libby writing to me.'

'How very convenient,' he drawled. 'You housekeep and tend the gardens—but what does my niece do to while away the hours? We're talking here about a girl who isn't happy unless she's surrounded by a free-loading mob of lunatics; a girl who, twice in her life, has had to be rescued by this terrible family of hers from dubious, if not downright dangerous, communes in which she got herself involved!'

'I know about that,' said Ginny uneasily, remembering Libby's own retrospective horror and shame when she had confided those episodes to her only a few months ago. 'And she's only too aware of what you saved her from. . . You see, Libby's changed; she's——'

'If she's changed so much,' he cut in savagely, 'how come she takes off the moment I arrive?'

'She hasn't taken off,' protested Ginny wretchedly, wondering how much of this she could take. 'She had already gone when you arrived!'

'So why did you feel obliged to call her and warn her I was here?'

'For heaven's sake, *she* rang *me*! groaned Ginny. 'Simply to say she didn't know how long she'd be staying on in Paris.'

'Oh yeah?' he drawled, imbuing the words with every bit as much scepticism as his niece did whenever she used them.

'Perhaps it won't surprise you to hear that, even had she not intended staying in Paris—which she had—she probably would have once I told her you were here,' retorted Ginny, as her wits at last began collecting themselves. 'I got the impression that you weren't exactly her favourite person.'

'And I guess I can't exactly be yours either,' he murmured, flashing her an unexpected smile. 'I shouldn't be taking out my feelings over family problems on an innocent bystander—especially not one who's served me up such a delightful meal.'

Ginny gave him a wary look, dazzled by the smile, yet not entirely convinced there hadn't been a measure of sarcasm in his softly spoken words.

'And now that we're on the subject, I have a proposition to put to you.' He gave a throaty chuckle as Ginny's eyes widened in consternation. 'I know they say the way to a man's heart is through his stomach,' he laughed, 'but that's not the sort of proposition I had in mind.'

Ginny maintained a mortified silence, wondering how on earth she could be expected to feed this man a string of lies when she was so easily caught off her guard.

'I keep you on as housekeeper and gardener—and you help me mend my bridges with Libby. You see, she's probably not aware that about a year ago I took over the European side of the family business—my base is now Paris.'

Libby was most certainly not aware that there was a member of the Grant family on the same continent, let alone a few hundred miles up the road from here, thought Ginny, her heart plummeting.

'Now that I'm settled in Paris, I've decided to combine a vacation with a look at our banking connections in the south. No doubt I'll have to make the odd trip or two back to Paris, but, for the next month, I'll be based here.'

'You. . .' began Ginny, and had to clear her throat when she discovered her mouth was bone-dry. 'You'll be staying here for a month?'

'That's what I said,' he replied, the heavily lashed midnight blue of his eyes drilling through her. 'Does the idea disturb you, Ginny?'

'What a strange thing to say!' she blustered, but what should have been a careless laugh came out as a strangled croak.

'Right,' he stated briskly. 'I'll let the agents know I'm here and they can arrange for extra staff for laundry and housework—I don't intend overworking you. As I see it, the only extra work for you will be cooking for three instead of two once Libby gets back.'

'Fine,' managed Ginny, so limp with shock that she was astounded she had actually got the word out. Right now she had to accept she was in no fit state to absorb any of this, she warned herself. 'Would you like me to make fresh coffee?' she offered, her mind beginning to ease into the blank state that had become its refuge during the years of mental warfare with her aunt.

'No, this is fine,' he said, producing a smile that penetrated her blankness and forcefully revived the memory of her initial reaction to his stunning looks. 'But I wouldn't mind a cognac—you will join me, won't you?' he asked, rising.

Thrown by her reaction to what, after all, had only been a smile, she decided she would join him, despite the fact that she rarely drank spirits. . . A cognac might be just what her strung-out nerves needed.

But after her first few sips of the fierily velvet spirit she found herself wondering if it wasn't over-stimulating her awareness as she began feeling she was hearing the odd note of mockery creeping into the tone of his desultory, though studiously polite conversation. Though it might have nothing to do with the cognac, she reasoned uncertainly, because even in the best of circumstances he wasn't the sort of man in whose company she would ever have felt in the least relaxed. And it wasn't simply his scarcely credible looks, it was everything else about him—from the almost arrogant ease oozing from his every pore to the careless expensiveness of every stitch he wore—that made him the sort of person who left her feeling gauche and vaguely inadequate.

'I'm sure that drive from Paris must have been tiring,' exclaimed Ginny, rising also and reaching over to collect the coffee-cups. 'I'm sure I'd have——' She let out a gasp of horror as she knocked a heavy crystal glass off the table. 'Oh, heavens!' she groaned, sinking to her knees and attempting to pick up pieces of the shattered glass. 'I'm so sorry!'

'For God's sake, what do you think you're doing?'

he exclaimed impatiently, striding over and hauling her to her feet. 'You'll cut yourself!'

'I really am sorry,' she muttered dazedly.

'So you broke a glass—it's no big deal.'

But a glass, judging by the weight and feel of it, that probably cost a small fortune, she fretted, her head beginning to swim. 'I'll replace it—I promise.'

'I'm not too sure about that,' he said, something in his tone drawing Ginny's eyes to his. She had thought for an instant he had been about to laugh, but there was no trace of laughter in either his expression or his tone as he continued. 'You see, that was one of a set, made exclusively for my great-great-grandfather—I guess they could be described as priceless.'

Ginny felt herself slump weakly against the table.

'So. . .I don't think you'll be replacing it in any hurry.'

This time when she looked up at him, she actually caught a glimpse of amusement on his face, before it instantly disappeared—or had she imagined it?

'I. . . This isn't your idea of a joke, is it?' she asked uncertainly.

'Of course it is,' he groaned exasperatedly. 'But it riled me the way you were carrying on as though the darned glass really had been priceless.'

'You have an extremely warped sense of humour,' she retorted with as much dignity as she could muster.

'You know something, Ginny?' he drawled. 'I've a feeling I'm really going to enjoy my stay here—what with my warped humour and——' He broke off, frowning as he leaned forward and peered down into her face.

'What is it?' she exclaimed, alarmed.

'Just indulging my warped humour,' he murmured, taking her by the shoulders and drawing her closer to him. 'I'm beginning to wonder if I didn't make the wrong proposition to you earlier,' he added huskily, lowerng his head towards hers.

Her entire body stiffened as his lips touched, then gently stirred against hers. Her first thought was to wonder where, exactly, she should attack him; her second was that it might not be such a good idea to attack any part of someone of his build. And then there was the fact that he wasn't using the slightest force as his mouth played in soft invitation against hers and that all she had to do was step back to escape. But at some point during those thoughts, her own lips had parted in a manner that could only be described as inviting, and her arms had somehow become entwined around his neck. And it was then, and only then, that his arms encircled her, drawing her body fully against the muscled leanness of his. It wasn't until a hint of demand entered his kiss that she began fighting—not the man, but the sensuous softness slinking insidiously throughout her entire being.

'You took your time deciding to spurn me,' he mocked softly as he released her, but there was a slight breathlessness to his words and a trace of bemusement in his eyes.

'That's because I shouldn't drink!' she exclaimed, then cringed at having come out with so pathetic an excuse.

'Yes, and you were really knocking it back,' he murmured. 'You must have had—well, all of two sips, by my reckoning.'

'I. . . What I meant was. . .'

'No, Ginny, the damage has already been done to my ego,' he sighed, walking towards the veranda doors. 'I'm sure that if I ever took the liberty of trying to kiss you again, I'd get an instant brush-off. . . And leave that broken glass alone, I'll see to it in the morning—I don't want you going anywhere near it in your drunken state.'

CHAPTER TWO

WHY she had assumed she would feel any better, having made a phone call to Libby during her visit to the market, was beyond her, thought Ginny irritably. She placed the last of her purchases in the basket of the bicycle she had found rusting in a shed at the villa soon after she had arrived, and climbed on to it.

Of course, she should have known she would end up lying to Libby, she mused dejectedly as she rode along. There had always been a mutually protective element in their relationship which, on her own part, had gone into overdrive now that Libby was pregnant.

'Ginny, just get the first train you can up here,' had been Libby's reaction to the news of the length of her uncle's proposed stay. 'Jeanne has plenty of space and can't wait to meet you.'

'And then we'd lose the money Michael's paying, not to mention what we get from my odd gardening contracts—Libby, we can't afford it.'

Not that long ago it had been a source of hilarity between them, thought Ginny wryly—Libby's being an heiress and their having to count every penny. But it had been only within the past month that Libby had managed to pay off the small fortune in debts that had littered her life, and now all her generous monthly allowance, together with anything they had left over from their strict budget, was set aside to cover the birth and any related expenses that might crop up—and they kept cropping up.

Of course she had lied, she thought wearily, oblivious of the azure blue of the sea now coming into view, a sight which usually filled her with peace and contentment. Last night, for the first time she could remember, she had gone to bed, her mind and body churning and reeling from the after-effects of what had only been a kiss: this morning she had woken to the same sensation—and it had frightened the wits out of her. . . Which was one of the reasons it had seemed safer, when talking to Libby, to weave a tale of a pleasantly courteous man who had apologised for the fact that he would be far too engrossed in business matters to be able to pass more than the time of day with her, and who had shown mercifully little interest in his absent niece.

'That could be the lull before the storm,' Libby had warned, plainly not altogether convinced. 'You wait till he gets suspicious and starts turning on the charm.'

It was at that point she had panicked into embroidering with a vengeance. 'You needn't worry on the charm score—there's some woman he's forever on the phone to. If I'm not mistaken, he's in love and I've a feeling she's going to join him any day.'

'Wow, Mikey in love!' Libby had gasped, unwittingly dispelling Ginny's immediate panic but also confirming her suspicion that Libby, despite her protestations to the contrary, retained a great deal of affection for her uncle. 'What I wouldn't give to see what she's like! But it's still not going to be that easy for you. I'll do what I can from this end, calling and speaking to him from time to time, but, like all the Grants, he has a very suspicious nature where I'm concerned. To be honest, if you had uppped and left, as I suggested, I'd not have put it past him to get the cops out looking for me.'

Ginny cycled up the drive and round to the back of the house.

'Where have you been?'

Almost falling from the bike with fright, she turned and flung a mutinous look in the direction of the scowling Michael Grant.

'I really don't think it's any of your business where I've been,' she retorted, wheeling the bike to the side of one of the garden sheds.

'As I see it, it's very much my business,' he snapped, dogging her footsteps. 'I employ you, don't I?'

'Indeed you do,' she replied, her tone saccharin-sweet while her blood boiled; this she most certainly could do without. 'But I wasn't sure that entailed my reporting my every move to you. But, if you must know, I was at the market, buying the food necessary for the meals my employment requires me to cook for you.'

'Fine, that's all I needed to know.'

Ginny flung the bicycle against the shed, fury making her reckless. 'But this afternoon I shall be elsewhere,' she announced, unloading the basket. 'Yours isn't the only garden I tend.'

'Well, it is now.'

'I beg your pardon?' she enquired icily, while a frantic voice inside her asked just what she thought she was doing. The fact that she hadn't any other gardening lined up was neither here nor there—her utter stupidity in even mentioning that she did other work was beyond belief.

'I think you heard well enough,' he informed her in steely tones. 'But if you want to play dumb, Ginny, dumb is what we'll play. So tell me, how many hours would you say constitute a full day's work?'

She had asked for this, she berated herself angrily, and she would no doubt get it in full.

'Eight,' she muttered.

'I'll be generous and call it seven. . . Now, by my reckoning, your only free time from working for me would be between the hours of ten at night and eight in the morning and I don't imagine too many folks would be lining up to have their gardens messed with during those hours.'

'I don't *mess* with gardens,' Ginny informed him frigidly, 'and anyway, I was only joking.'

'Glad to hear it,' he drawled, his eyes flickering with barely concealed disdain over her dungaree-clad figure before he turned and walked towards the house. 'We need to talk,' he called over his shoulder, 'so how about if you make us some coffee so we can do it in comfort?'

And how about if you took a running jump? fumed Ginny to herself, convinced he intended complaining about her appearance. What had he in mind—decking her out in a uniform?

Muttering angrily to herself, and convinced she wouldn't survive two hours of this treatment, let alone a whole month of it, she took herself off to the kitchen. But at least some good had come out of this ghastly encounter, she thought, calming a little as she put her purchases away. Her lying awake half the night racked by memories of being kissed by him had been no more than a stress-induced mental aberration—that was for sure.

She got out coffee-beans and the grinder, her moment of relief swiftly dissipating into frustration. She was beginning to feel as though she had a terrible weight on her shoulders. Libby seemed to thrive on intrigue, whereas she simply wasn't cut out for it.

Perhaps it was because Libby's background was so steeped in wealth that she had such a cavalier attitude towards money.

'OK, so I'll pay it all back once I come into my inheritance,' Libby had laughed, when Ginny had balked at the idea of their claiming the two salaries—and in Ginny's name—from the villa. 'No sweat.'

The idea had disturbed her then, thought Ginny miserably, and now it made her shrivel with embarrassment every time she thought about it. If Michael had fired her on the spot, or threatened her with legal action, she couldn't honestly have blamed him. But her guilt in that respect didn't alter the fact that his gallingly high-handed attitude was touching a particularly raw spot in her; she had had enough of being treated like an unpaid skivvy by her aunt ever to take it again—and especially not from this over-prvileged, autocratic American!

'What are you doing—growing the beans for that coffee?'

Ginny responded to those words from a few paces behind her with a jump that sent the coffee she had just ground scattering everywhere.

'Now look what you've made me do!' she exclaimed accusingly. 'I'll have to grind more!'

'I'll grind—you clear up that mess,' drawled Michael.

'Excuse me,' hissed Ginny, her hackles rising, 'I might be employed by you, but would you mind not issuing me orders as though I were some sort of serf?'

'OK. *Please*, Ginny, I'd be terribly grateful if you'd clear up the mess you've just made,' he murmured in a grating parody of an English accent. 'Tell me, are you always this sensitive?'

Ginny's unladylike retort was drowned by the shriek

of the coffee-grinder he switched on just as she uttered it.

'You've over-filled it!' she yelled over the din.

'What?'

'I said. . . Oh, forget it!'

He switched off the grinder. 'I couldn't hear you with that thing on. Does it always make that noise?' he enquired, his expression over-brimming with puzzled innocence.

'Only when it's too full,' snapped Ginny, flashing him her most withering look before finishing clearing up the mess and then returning to making the coffee.

'Things have been happening here since you've been out,' he said.

Ginny had to force herself to keep on with what she was doing as she felt herself freeze. He had found out about Libby!

'The equipment I'll need to work from here arrived—I'm using the library as an office.'

'Where do you want to drink this?' asked Ginny, relief unfreezing her as she turned towards him with the coffee-jug.

'Here will do fine,' he replied, making no attempt to lend a hand as he took a seat at the table. 'Have you any office experience?'

Ginny, who had been just about to pour the coffee, gave him a look of frowning suspicion. 'A little,' she muttered, and all of it bad, she added to herself as she poured out two cups. 'Why?' she asked, handing him one.

'I thought you could help me out with a bit of office work—answering the telephone and checking the odd computer print-out with me.'

'Oh, I see—you'd like me to work for you twenty-one hours a day, is that it?'

There was a mixture of irritation and amusement on his face as he took a sip from his mug.

'No, it would involve so little time that I planned letting you off cleaning my shoes in lieu,' he drawled. 'So, how about it?'

'With an organisation as vast as yours is reputed to be, I'd have thought you'd have a battalion of experts, not to mention clerical staff, at your beck and call.'

'And you'd have thought right,' he said. 'But, remember, a year ago I was very much the new guy here. Now I'm the not-so-new guy and I feel the time has come for me to take a couple of steps back and see what sort of picture I get of the overall scene.'

In other words, thought Ginny, whatever he was doing here, he didn't want his Paris staff knowing about it. . . A somewhat different story from the one he had originally given her.

Irritation flashed across his features. 'All you have to do is say yes or no.'

'I'd be happy to,' stated Ginny, her curiosity aroused, 'but I'm afraid I wouldn't be much use—I speak hardly any French.'

'I guess that could present one or two problems, but I still might be able to use you. Libby's French is OK—perhaps she might help me out if the need arises. When did you say she'd be back?'

'I didn't,' replied Ginny, her curiosity giving way to an almost sickening feeling of apprehension. 'I've already told you, I don't know.' And how many more times was he going to ask her that same question?

'I guess you don't think she'd be too happy to help me out in an office or anywhere else,' he said quietly. 'Libby and I, as you know, aren't exactly buddies right now, but it wasn't always like that. And once she would have jumped at helping out. When she was still quite a small kid, I took her to visit my brother, David, at his office. She was fascinated by the whole set-up and afterwards asked me some pretty adult questions about the family business,' he continued, his tone surprising Ginny in that it sounded almost wistful. 'I told her all I could, which wasn't a great deal as I'd only just started at Princeton and was still pretty ignorant of the set-up myself. Years later, when I'd taken my place as an executive director, I found myself remembering all those questions she had asked—but by then it was too late.'

'In what way?'

'Because she'd embarked on a career of screwing up her life in whatever way she could,' he snapped. 'Look, I'm not claiming she had an easy time of it—Jack Collier may be in a class of his own as an academic, but he sure as hell was a lousy father.'

'That may be so, but Libby seems to love him—warts and all,' stated Ginny. Even in the rare moments when Libby had actually railed against her mixed-up father, there had been no mistaking her exasperated love for him. 'Which is more than can be said for her feelings towards the Grant family.'

'I'd be the last to deny the Grants have their faults,' conceded Michael. 'Though I'd say mine is pretty much the same as any other family—and not necessarily American—with what some might describe as an over-abundance of wealth and influence. Being the typical patriarch of such a family, my father can be pretty difficult to get on with at times—but my brother's a much softer character.'

Ginny took a quick gulp from her cup to mask her surprise: she had somehow gained the impression that Libby regarded her uncle David as something of an ogre.

'I've a feeling Libby's always resented David and his wife once trying to get custody of her. The only reason they even contemplated such a step was because they loved her and felt the way Jack was diving in and out of marriages couldn't be doing her any good. Once they lost the case we rarely saw Libby, though whether that was coincidence or revenge on her father's part is anyone's guess.'

'I'm afraid I can't help you there,' said Ginny, who knew nothing of the incident, but the feelings of sympathy stirring in her made her uneasy. 'Libby's never gone into much detail about her family problems.' Though even when she had been quite young, Ginny had often wondered if love hadn't been the driving force behind the Grant family's interference, about which Libby sometimes complained with such bitterness.

'If you say so,' he drawled sceptically.

'I *do* say so,' snapped Ginny, his tone dissipating much of her discomfiting compassion. 'Ours would have been a pretty depressing friendship if the two of us had spent our time exchanging the details of our mutual woes!'

'Oh, so you're also a bundle of woes, are you, Ginny?' he enquired, his tone sarcastic rather than sympathetic.

'You said you wanted to talk to me,' snapped Ginny, any sympathy she had felt now entirely dissipated.

'I did—and that's what I was under the impression I was doing,' he muttered, stretching, then dragging his fingers absent-mindedly through his hair. 'Perhaps I'm just kidding myself, hoping that Libby and I can spend time together, and wondering if I could make a start on answering some of those questions she asked all those years ago.'

'I thought you'd decided it was too late,' retorted Ginny, still rattled and on edge.

'You're the one who insists she's turned over a new leaf,' he snapped.

'And she has,' protested Ginny, feeling more and more trapped. Her only alternative to arousing his anger and suspicion was to trot out words that lent credence to the lie that Libby was going to show up, but now her own innate sense of fairness was getting in the way of such words.

'But not enough for her to want to mend her bridges with her family,' he stated grimly.

'No—that isn't true!' blurted out Ginny. Even if there hadn't been Libby's oft-proclaimed intention to make her peace with the Grants once she and Jean-Claude were married, there was the undeniable affection Libby still felt for Michael—there had been no mistaking it in her voice this morning.

'Well, I dare say I'll be able to judge that for myself soon enough,' he muttered, rising and going over to pour himself more coffee. 'Would you like more?'

Ginny shook her head, searching frantically for something non-contentious to say. 'I'm sure Libby probably would be interested in learning more about the family business,' she eventually managed.

'Probably,' he agreed, an edge of sarcasm in his tone. 'Especially the financial side of it, which is what I deal with. Given that her trust benefits considerably from it annually, it could be said she has quite an interest in it already.' He returned to his seat, his expression oddly diffident as he glanced across at her. 'I don't have any idea how much you really know about the sort of things Libby got up to,' he muttered. 'But no matter how we tried to answer what all the psychologists kept saying were her cries for help—and

I admit they were sometimes answered very clumsily—we couldn't get through to her. I was just a kid when her mother died. . .but I loved my big sister—and Libby's all I, and the rest of my family, have left of her.'

It was the terrible reminder of the contrasting lack of love in her aunt that brought the sudden sting of tears to Ginny's eyes and made her even more inclined to believe that, high-handed though their dealings with Libby had always been, the Grants truly had been motivated by love.

'I promise you. . .Libby has really changed,' she said in a slightly muffled voice.

'I look forward to seeing that for myself,' he muttered.

Ginny took another sip of her now cold coffee, trying desperately to harden herself against the guilt niggling inside her by reminding herself of how he had landed himself in Libby's bad books in the first place.

'And I look forward to getting to know you, Ginny,' he added after a pause, his intensely blue eyes rising to hers, scattering her thoughts and re-igniting those disturbing memories that only a while ago she had so blithely dismissed as mental aberration. 'It's not often I get the chance to meet with Libby's friends.'

Perhaps not, thought Ginny, anger stirring once more in her, but from what Libby had said, he had made a point of getting to know one in particular most intimately.

She rose and, without a word, poured herself more coffee, most of the anger in her directed at herself. All right, so she had found him attractive before Libby had warned her what he was like, but that wasn't an excuse for the way she was behaving now—in fact, there was something bordering on the unhealthy in the way that she could be actively disliking him one moment and feeling violently attracted to him the next.

'You're unusually silent, Ginny,' he murmured, his words coming from right behind her and making her start with fright. 'Does that mean you don't want me to get to know you?'

'I. . . No,' she stammered, striving to get a grip on herself. 'You frightened the life out of me, creeping up on me like that!'

'I'm sorry. The last thing I meant to do was frighten you,' he said, placing an apparently concerned arm around her shoulder. 'And isn't that a good reason for us getting to know one another. . .to ensure neither of us feels afraid of the other?'

'Oh, yes—I'm sure you're terrified out of your wits by me,' retorted Ginny, stepping back against the counter as she shrugged his arm from her shoulder. His arm slid down and repositioned itself against her back.

'Have I reason to be?' he asked softly, his arm tightening against her back and drawing her towards him.

'Don't!' she warned through clenched teeth, her hands rising and pressing against his chest.

'Don't what, Ginny?' he laughed softly. 'I honestly haven't decided what I'm going to do with you yet.'

'Well, don't try seducing me the way you did that other friend of Libby's because it's not going to work on me!'

The softness of laughter was stripped from his face, leaving instead a harsh mask of coldness.

'So Libby warned you about me, did she?' he enquired icily.

'Yes, she did. And if you——'

'I wonder what it is she's so frightened I'm going to get out of you?' he asked in that same frigid tone.

'She's not frightened you'll get anything out of me,' exclaimed Ginny, panic swamping her as she realised just what she had said.

'So why did she feel it necessary to warn you?' he demanded, his hands now fiercely gripping the tops of her arms and making any thought of escape a waste of time.

'I. . . Because. . . You're hurting me!'

'I'm sorry,' he muttered, releasing her, but leaving her trapped against the counter. 'Now answer my question.'

'She warned me because of me—not because of you,' replied Ginny hoarsely, wishing the ground would open up and swallow her.

'Am I supposed to make sense of that?' he snapped, his tall body tensing with anger.

'Libby was afraid I'd find you attractive,' ground out Ginny, her cheeks flaming with mortification. 'I. . . She thinks I'm—that I tend to be attracted to the wrong sort of men.'

'So she obviously thought I'd find your neo-Huckleberry Finn appeal irresistible,' he drawled, 'otherwise she wouldn't have felt obliged to warn you.'

'No!' protested Ginny, her entire being awash with humiliation. 'I. . . She said there was a lot about me that was like that other friend of hers. . . She just felt she should warn me.'

'You're nothing like that poor, unfortunate creature I'm rumoured to have used so abominably,' he stated callously. 'If I remember right, she didn't slop around the place in dungarees all the time and I didn't have any problem working out whether she was male or female the first time I set eyes on her. And she——'

'You didn't seem to have any doubts which I was when you made a lunge for me after dinner last night!' exploded Ginny, beside herself with rage.

'By then you had your party gear on—denims and a T-shirt, wasn't it?' he drawled. 'Though perhaps you wouldn't remember, given the drunken state it seems you were in.'

Choking back a squeal of outrage, Ginny made to push her way past him. 'Get out of my way!' she hissed when he blocked her path.

'What's up, Ginny?' he grinned down at her.

'Just get out of my way!' she shrieked. 'What sort of a man are you? How could you possibly kiss someone you find as revolting as you do me?'

'Believe me, Ginny, I'd feel a lot happier if I did find you revolting.'

'I. . . What's that supposed to mean?' she demanded, gazing up with hostility into a pair of laughing blue eyes and finding, to her utter horror, excitement fluttering through her.

'I'm not too sure,' he answered with a wry smile. 'Though it does seem Libby's right in one respect—I'm sure you'll agree, you'd feel a lot safer if you found me revolting.'

'I hate to disillusion you,' exclaimed Ginny furiously, 'but I feel perfectly safe.' Talk about rubbing her nose in it!

'Oh yeah?' he drawled with a humourless laugh. 'So it really was that half teaspoon of cognac, and not my irresistible appeal, that stirred your libido last night.'

'Haven't you work to do?' enquired Ginny frigidly, sidling along the edge of the counter away from the bulk of his body. 'I know I have.'

'If you want me to get out of your way,' he murm.ıred innocently, reaching out and pulling her against him, 'all you have to do is say.'

Ginny made no attempt to escape; instead she concentrated all her energies on not moving so much as a muscle for fear of betraying the lazy, throbbing warmth with which her body was responding to contact with his.

It was he who moved, his arms tightening around her, a protesting groan of disbelief escaping him as desire surged hotly through his lean body.

Then his mouth was on hers, hard and demanding, while his tongue sought the succulent depths behind her parted lips.

Her absolute certainty that what was erupting between them was too explosively spontaneous ever to have been planned by him so side-tracked her mind that thought of resistance never once entered it. She wasn't conscious of reaching up on tiptoes to entwine her arms around his neck; she was merely responding to the pounding need awakened in her to mould her body ever closer to the enticing heat of his. And the only protest that escaped her, when his hands reached beneath the bagginess of her dungarees and began an impatient search of her trembling body, was at the restrictions imposed on those hands.

He drew her from him, his lips murmuring their impatience even as they remained locked in passionate turmoil with hers, while his hands gave up their attempts to cup her throbbing breasts and reached instead for the fastenings that would free them.

'I can't see what I'm doing,' he groaned barely coherently, dragging his mouth reluctantly from hers. 'Ginny, I. . . Oh, hell,' he rasped, the words ragged with disbelief as sanity began imposing itself on him.

Ginny heard her own gasp of utter incredulity as her

arms slid lifelessly from around the body to which they had been clinging with such uninhibited fervour.

'So, you feel perfectly safe, do you?' he demanded almost angrily, then gave a dazed shake of his head. 'Forget I said that,' he muttered brusquely, turning abruptly from her.

'Why?' demanded Ginny recklessly, her body still on fire from the feel of his, her mind spinning from the futility of the denials she was trying to impose on it. 'OK, so I was wrong! But at least I have the excuse of being a lousy judge of men—what's yours?'

'I don't have any excuse,' he informed her icily as he strode towards the door. 'But once I hear from the people I have investigating you, I should have a much better idea of what I'm up against.'

CHAPTER THREE

'GINNY!'

Ginny's entire body froze for an instant, then she continued hoeing the geranium bed, the stark white gleam of her knuckles against the handle the only outward sign of an inner fury.

That bellowed name was one of only a handful of words to have broken the silence that had descended like a wall between them since his announcement that he was having her investigated. Quite frankly, she couldn't have cared less if they'd never exchanged another word for the rest of their lives, she told herself, hoeing like one possessed. And if he really expected her to believe his ridiculous claim, he must think her the biggest fool alive—the only information he had on her was her name, for heaven's sake!

'Ginny, I called you,' exclaimed Michael exasperatedly, striding towards her. 'Didn't you hear me?'

'I'm sure the whole region heard you.'

'So how come you didn't answer me?'

'Because, believe it or not, I'm not a dog trained to respond to your every command,' she retortedly hotly, glowering up at him as his narrowed eyes flickered coolly over her dishevelled appearance.

'You were some distance away, so I called loudly,' he stated unconcernedly. 'If you chose to interpret it differently, that's your problem. Anyway, I wanted to tell you Libby called—and that I'm hungry.'

Ginny tried to counteract the shock surging through her by reminding herself that Libby had said that she would ring him and that her only reason for concern would have been had Libby not done so.

'I. . . You were in your ofice so early this morning, I didn't know what to do about breakfast,' she stammered.

'And it didn't occur to you to ask me?'

Though he injected a questioning lilt into those mocking words, Ginny treated them as the statement they were obviously intended to be, and ignored them. 'There's bread and some goat's cheese—or I could cook some——'

'Bread and cheese will do me fine,' he cut in, his eyes meeting hers in a look of chilling balefulness. 'Get yourself cleaned up and we'll eat together.'

'I'm not hungry,' retorted Ginny, willing herself not to be intimidated by those eyes.

'I'd like you to join me, anyway,' he stated, then turned and strode back towards the house.

Ginny flung down the hoe, her blood boiling—an effect he managed to have on her just about every time he opened that supercilious mouth of his, she noted with outrage. Except that it wasn't always anger with which he made her blood boil, she reminded herself with a jolt of alarm that deflated her rage like a pricked balloon. She tensed as a now almost familiar honeyed warmth began slinking its way seductively through her. She wasn't normally susceptible to looks, no matter how devastating, she reasoned exasperatedly, and especially not when they cloaked a personality as vile as Michael Grant's did.

With a groan of pure vexation at her own stupidity, she ran to the house and raced upstairs to her room.

She couldn't have it both ways, she argued impatiently with herself as she took a quick shower; despairing one minute of her apparent inability to feel anything more than a mild flutter of attraction towards a man, and wallowing in *angst* the next because one of them was affecting her in a manner she hadn't bargained for.

Her look was brooding as she slipped on a fresh white T-shirt, a leaden heat throbbing through her as her mind attempted to skirt the passion that had flared between them the day before in order to examine his reaction to what had happened. She walked over to the wardrobe and opened its doors. Perhaps a really calculating man could have produced to order that groan of surprised disbelief that had escaped him. . . but never the accompanying desire that had surged hot and unmistakable in his body.

Never before in her life had any man had the power to reduce her to this mind-sapping state of permanent confusion—though what little she knew about men was probably dangerous, she reflected bitterly. Her trouble was that her aunt's vituperative hounding of her over her first and only sexual experience wasn't the only price she had paid for that oddly innocent indiscretion—ever since that incident it had been as though she had been trapped in an emotional time-warp, simply marking time until. . . She gave a violent shake of her head, dragging a navy skirt from the wardrobe and putting it on.

But her actions did nothing to stem the turbulent flow of her thoughts. No, this most certainly wasn't what she had bargained for, she told herself as she finished doing up her skirt—this ghastly state of being intermittently racked by hot, stomach-churning, unadulterated lust for a man she had difficulty liking, let alone loving!

She walked to the door, but instead of opening it,

she slumped against it, giggling weakly as a picture of her aunt's forbidding face leapt to her mind.

'A shock though all this may be to me,' she whispered aloud to her absent aunt, 'it certainly wouldn't come as one to you.'

Halfway down the stairs, she was still having difficulty composing herself. There was nothing in the least amusing about this and her behaviour was verging on being hysterical, she rebuked herself sternly, but she was still grinning when she entered the kitchen.

'You look mighty amused,' scowled Michael, when she entered the kitchen. 'Care to share the joke?'

'I doubt if you'd appreciate it,' replied Ginny, on the verge of another fit of the giggles as she walked over to the dresser and got down crockery.

'Try me.'

Ginny almost choked trying not to imagine his likely reaction. Composing her features, she took the crockery to the table and found her hilarity turning swiftly to resentment. Even with a face like a thundercloud, she thought exasperatedly, he still looked disgustingly attractive. . . And she was out of her mind to think she had anything to laugh about!

'I guess the same could be said about the joke bugging me right now,' he muttered morosely, taking a seat at the table. 'You wouldn't appreciate it either.'

'I thought jokes were meant to amuse rather than annoy people,' retorted Ginny, placing the food on the table and noting, with surprise, that he had actually made a pot of coffee. Obviously the effort expended had drained him of the last vestiges of his mercurial charm, she thought waspishly as she returned to the fridge and got out a jug of fresh lemon for herself.

'Well, this one's annoying me,' he growled, helping himself to a chunk of bread, then watching her through coldly narrowed eyes as, still standing, she poured herself a glass of lemon. 'That's pretty addictive, that stuff,' he remarked unexpectedly, eyeing the jug of lemon. 'You'd better get a supply of it in—I'd hate to run out of it.'

'I don't have to get it in,' replied Ginny, slightly nonplussed by his sudden switch, 'I make it myself.'

'A woman of infinite talent,' he drawled, and placed some cheese next to the bread on his plate.

Ginny watched him, memories of the innumerable clashes she had had with her aunt flashing through her mind, and with them the startled realisation that in all those years she had never once experienced the violently murderous thoughts now filling her head. But then, her aunt had always been consistently unpleasant, whereas the only consistent thing about Michael's moods were their inconsistency.

'As I said,' she stated, her words wooden with her determination not to betray the state to which she had been so swiftly reduced. 'I'm not hungry and I've several things to be getting——'

'Sit down!' he roared, slamming his palm against the table for emphasis.

Ginny stiffened with shock. 'I think you'd better find yourself another gardener and housekeeper,' she stated hoarsely. 'I've had enough of this.'

'OK, I'm sorry—I didn't mean to yell like that,' he muttered, rising to his feet and walking to her side. 'Come and sit down—we need to talk.'

'No, we don't need to talk,' exclaimed Ginny, backing away from him as she spoke. 'There's nothing for us to talk about—I'm leaving!'

'There are a number of reasons why you won't be leaving, Ginny,' he stated quietly, 'the main one being that Libby says she'll be back the day after tomorrow.'

Ginny's eyes flew to his; blue consternation-filled eyes meeting an impenetrable wall of navy.

'Yes,' he murmured, the light touch of his hand against her shoulder guiding her towards a chair, 'I thought you'd be relieved to hear that.'

Ginny sat down, her mind too preoccupied even to contemplate resistance.

'Though I was a little surprised,' he was continuing relentlessly, as he returned to the chair opposite her, 'that you didn't even ask what she had to say, when I told you she'd called—or rather, when you showed no interest at all in the fact that she had called.'

She had over-reacted by under-reacting, Ginny realised with a growing sense of helplessness—because she was useless at anything approaching subterfuge.

'Anyway—about your leaving,' he murmured, pouring himself coffee, 'I think you'll find that the contract you signed with my agent stipulates a month's notice.'

It probably did, thought Ginny miserably, remembering her disquiet on discovering she would actually be required to sign a contract, and Libby's laughing dismissal of her qualms.

'But I'm a reasonable guy. I wouldn't hold you to that if you really wanted to leave. I'll make a real effort not to yell at you till Libby gets back. But, once she's here, if you still feel you want to leave, you're free to go. Now that's a pretty fair deal, isn't it?'

Ginny noded, her lowered eyes refusing to meet his for fear of what they would encounter. It wasn't a fair deal and she had a nasty feeling he knew so. All right, so he couldn't be as certain as she was that Libby wouldn't be arriving. . .but that must be the joke to which he had so grimly referred. It was the thought of how he would react once that joke was out in the open that filled her with a cold dread—a dread heightened by an inescapable tinge of guilt.

'I wonder if you'll be as relieved as I shall when Libby finally shows up,' he said quietly.

'Why should I be relieved?' asked Ginny guardedly, the note almost of wistfulness in his words, despite their deliberate toying with her, magnifying her guilt. 'You make it sound as though she's been in some sort of danger—all she's doing is visiting friends in Paris.'

'For once, that wasn't what I meant,' he said. 'I was referring to the bad start we got off to because of her absence.'

Ginny gazed sightlessly down into the glass clasped tightly in both her hands, completely taken aback by his words. But it wasn't just his words, she thought miserably, and it wasn't just that she felt uncomfortable with all this deceit. This was like being on an emotional roller-coaster, not knowing from one moment to the next how he was going to affect her. Guilt, hatred, compassion, lust. . . She had every right to be frightened out of her wits.

'I guess I'm trying to say I'm sorry for the way I've been behaving,' he said quietly, 'especially as I know nothing about you. . . Tell me about yourself.'

'So that you can check it against what your spies report on me?' demanded Ginny, in a desperate attempt to counteract what was happening to her.

'I guess I asked for that,' he muttered, a mixture of lingering suspicion and desperation in the look he gave her. 'But given what you know about Libby, wouldn't you have you checked out if you were me?'

'Given what I know about Libby as she is now—no, I wouldn't,' sighed Ginny, her heart none the less going out to him.

'But I don't know the Libby you claim exists now,'

he said. 'All I have to go on is past experience. My brother was once conned into believing Libby had changed for the better. She'd changed, all right; she was well on the way to becoming a zombie in some freaked-out cult.'

'I'm not denying how confused Libby's been in the past and how badly she behaved,' protested Ginny. 'But I promise you, she's left that past behind for good. She realises how much she owes her family for rescuing her as they did.'

'The trouble is, that's what she said at the time,' retorted Michael grimly, 'then a year later got herself involved with an even more dangerous lot. So you see, Ginny, where Libby's concerned, what other people tell me doesn't count—I have to see for myself that she's OK.' He tilted back his chair, his eyes holding hers in open challenge. 'And I'll be able to do that the day after tomorrow—right?'

'Yes,' said Ginny, her eyes dropping from his while her stomach knotted sickeningly. 'And you'll be able to call your bloodhounds off me,' she added, in a desperate attempt to lighten the charged atmosphere.

'You have something to hide, do you, Ginny?' he enquired silkily.

'Of course I haven't!' she exclaimed indignantly, her fruitless stab at levity abandoned. 'And anyway, I'm not as stupid as you think,' she added fiercely. 'Even I know you can't investigate people without having a few basic facts about them.'

'Such as a name, passport number and last address in the UK?' he murmured. 'All the details you gave the agent after Libby had talked him into employing you.'

'Obviously I am as stupid as you think,' muttered Ginny, with the spontaneous candour of one thoroughly defeated, then gave a start of surprise when he burst out laughing.

'I'm not too sure what I think of you, but it certainly isn't that you're stupid,' he said, and gave her a smile that did things to her that both shocked and frightened her. 'Ginny, I meant it when I said I was sorry for the way I've been behaving,' he added quietly. 'And to prove I'm not always such a boor, how about if I take you out to dinner tonight? There's this great restaurant in—'

'I can't,' cut in Ginny, aghast. The last thing she could cope with was an evening out with this man on his best behaviour—she couldn't even trust herself when he was behaving badly! 'It's very kind of you. . . but I have a prior engagement.' The instant the lie was out she sensed his stiffening withdrawal.

'A prior engagement?' he enquired in sarcastic parody. 'Had you intended letting me know, or were you just going to slip out and surprise me?'

'Of course I was going to let you know,' she exclaimed, flustered. 'I. . . You needn't worry, I'll cook you something before I go.'

'Gee, that *is* a relief,' he drawled, his words dripping with sarcasm. 'But you needn't bother—I'll eat in Cannes. So tell me, Ginny,' he murmured, rising to his feet, his look salacious as it travelled the length of her body, 'who's the lucky guy?'

Ginny felt the colour drain from her face. 'I can't think why you bothered wasting your breath,' she exclaimed hoarsely.

'Wasting my breath?'

'Apologising for the way you behave—when you have no intention whatever of changing it.'

'You're wrong, Ginny,' he informed her icily, 'as far

as my behaviour goes. That's something I have every intention of changing.'

'I don't *want* a lift,' protested Ginny, for the second time in a space of minutes. She couldn't leave well alone, she accused herself frustratedly. Instead of letting him take off for Cannes and then simply going to bed early, she had had to embroider on her lie by making a show of leaving before he did. 'I *like* cycling!'

'I wasn't asking what you liked,' snapped Michael, scowling down at her. 'You can't go around on that thing in the dark. If you don't want me to know where you're going—OK; I'll call you a cab.'

'For heaven's sake!' she protested wearily. 'I've already told you—I'm meeting a friend at one of the cafés in the village, but I just don't happen to remember its name.'

'Fine—there's no reason why I shouldn't drop you off there,' he informed her through clenched teeth, then caught her by the arm and almost dragged her from the house. 'You can give me directions once we get into the village.'

There were several reasons why he shouldn't drop her off, thought Ginny in panic, tearing free her arm as they reached the car, one being that she was going to have a long walk back; and another being that she wouldn't put it past Michael to hang around to see who her fictitious date was. Why, oh, why hadn't she simply told him she didn't want to go out with him tonight?

'Do up your seatbelt,' he snapped, starting the car.

'Give me a chance!' she snapped back. 'And you can drop the hypocrisy concerning my safety.'

'Your safety is of paramount importance to me,' he informed her in saccharin tones as he turned out on to the road. 'I'd have to find someone else to feed me if a passing car knocked you off that antiquated contraption of a bike you were so keen to use. And I can't say I think much of your date—why can't he come and fetch you like any civilised guy would?'

'I don't see why you automatically leap to the conclusion it's a man I'm meeting,' retorted Ginny, then marvelled at her own stupidity—she might just as well invite him to hang around to find out.

'Well, if you're not, all I can say is that it's a waste of a beautiful evening,' he murmured.

'Is that so?'

'It sure is,' he replied, with a chuckle that had her clenching her hands in exasperated fury with herself because of the unsettling shiver of excitement it sent winging through her. 'Or doesn't a late fall evening in a place as beautiful as this bring out the romantic in you, Ginny?'

'Not particularly,' she muttered, then added sharply, 'Perhaps I'm not the romantic you so obviously are.'

'Sarcasm doesn't suit you, Ginny,' he chided, with another of those chuckles she found so appallingly disruptive. 'But, whether you believe it or not, I can be as romantic as the next guy. . .or so I try telling myself.'

'If you. . . What are you doing?' she exclaimed in alarm, as the car slewed over on to the grassy verge and jarred to a sudden halt.

'I want to show you something,' he replied, stepping from the car.

Michael, surely it can wait,' she protested as he opened her door. 'I—I'll be late.' She heard the sound of her words catching in her throat as he leaned in and undid her seatbelt, his torso brushing hers.

'No you won't—you'd planned on cycling, remember?' he murmured, taking her by the hand and drawing her from the car.

'This is ridiculous,' she fumed, dragging free her hand and watching in irate bemusement as his tall figure strolled to the far edge of the tree-lined grassy verge.

'Come over here,' he called to her. 'Right here next to me.'

Part of her refusing to believe this was happening, Ginny complied. She had saddled herself with the prospect of ordering, in a language she didn't speak, a meal she didn't want, followed by a cross-country trek back to the villa in the dark—and all to avoid the company of the man she was now alone with in the middle of nowhere!

So busy was she being annoyed over having landed herself in this ridiculous predicament, it barely registered with her when an arm descended across her shoulders and she was drawn close to his side.

'Look straight ahead through that gap in the trees,' he ordered, angling her head with the hand of the arm around her and pointing with his free hand, 'and out across the water.'

Her angry thoughts now dissipated by a stomach-churning awareness of the muscled body against which her own was now clamped, Ginny's gaze followed his directions.

'Now tell me,' he said softly, 'is that ridiculous—or just plain breathtaking?'

'It's beautiful,' she breathed in spontaneous awe, wondering just how and when he had managed to discover this precise spot, where the parting of the trees allowed so perfect a view of the moon's reflected light dancing in silvery softness across the surface of the sea. 'How on earth did you manage to find exactly this spot?' she asked, her thoughts spilling into words. At first she felt surprise when he began chuckling softly to himself; then she was squirming with the realisation of her own naïveté as she remembered his ambivalent references to romance. 'Ask a stupid question,' she muttered in irritation with herself, but found her attempts to draw away from him foiled by the swift pressure exerted by the arm still across her shoulders.

'I guess that was a pretty dumb question,' he chuckled. 'Or maybe it's just that you're more of a romantic than you're admitting to.'

'I beg your pardon?' gasped Ginny, completely thrown by his remark.

'I said——'

'I'm perfectly aware of what you said,' she snapped through his words, then added irritably, 'Look—why don't you stay here and admire the view? I'll walk the rest of the way!'

'Ginny, something's telling me we're operating on different wavebands here,' he said, the pressure of his arm increasing and forcing her round to face him. 'If I upset you by agreeing you asked a pretty dumb question——'

'Michael, I want to go—I'm going to be late!'

'We're still way ahead of your original schedule,' he pointed out unconcernedly. 'Ginny, surely I can't have bugged you like this just by suggesting you have a romantic streak in you?'

'You're the one claiming to be the romantic,' she rounded on him angrily. 'For all I know, you've a dozen or more such places up your sleeve and I——'

'Up my sleeve,' he mocked, with a rumbling laugh of disbelief. 'Ginny, I hate to disillusion you, but I've never stood in this spot in my life before,' he continued, the laughter still rumbling through his words.

'On a night like this and in a place like this, where you have trees, the sea and the moonlight, simple logic dictates that a decent gap in those trees will form a picture that's as near as damn it perfect.'

Ginny wished she could curl up and die. 'I—I suppose you're right,' she stammered, her lowered eyes trained resolutely on the breast pocket of his lightweight linen jacket.

'There's no supposing about it,' he retorted, cupping her face in his hands and tilting it upwards. 'Only a complete romantic would have difficulty accepting that the entire coastline's littered with views every bit as beautiful as this.'

'All right,' she snapped, her eyes still loath to meet his, 'you've made your point! Can we go now?'

'Ginny, why won't you look at me?'

'Because,' she began, her eyes instinctively rising to his. 'Because. . .' Her words petered away to nothing as the expression that flitted across the shadowed contours of his handsome face warned her he had read something in her eyes—an uncompromisingly explicit something that had brought about that fleeting look of triumph before his head lowered to hers.

Please don't let this be happening to me, she prayed in silent dread, as she felt her entire body leap in torrid response to the ardent probing of his mouth on hers. But it was happening to her—this sensation of being possessed body and soul that filled her as his arms closed around her—as it had been threatening to since that first time he had taken her in his arms.

Yet even as a soft moan escaped her, of protest that it should be in this man's arms that she should discover her own capacity for desire, her arms were instinctively reaching up and winding around his neck in spontaneous acquiescence. And then she was lost in the sensations bombarding her as his hands began skimming the slim contours of her unresisting body, their silken heat burning against her flesh through the light cotton of her dress.

'Come back home with me, Ginny,' he groaned against her parted lips, while his fingers nimbly undid the buttons at the front of her dress. 'There are only three eating places in town—we can call them all and tell him you can't make it.'

The cry that escaped her had nothing to do with the words she had barely heard; it was one of gasping reaction to the agonising pleasure that had begun rampaging through her when his hands slid beneath the flimsy lace of her bra to caress against her burning flesh.

'These damned clothes!' he protested huskily, then gave a chuckle of undisguised satisfaction as the impatient seduction of his hands against her tautly aroused breasts snapped the fragile lace beneath which they trespassed.

'Michael!' she choked, but there was no hint of censure in her tone as her body luxuriated in its sudden freedom to be explored without constraint.

'Have you any idea how much I want you?' he demanded hoarsely, moulding her pliant body to his in a suffocating closeness that left no room for doubt as to the intensity of his desire. 'Come home with me now, Ginny. . .before it's too late.'

'Too late?' she echoed distractedly, her hands sliding to his chest, her fingers trembling in their haste to undo the buttons of his shirt.

'Before I lose all sense of reason and make love to you right here!' he groaned, then pushed her forcefully from him. 'I'm sorry, honey,' he muttered unsteadily, dragging his hands impatiently through his hair as he took a step back from her, 'but I had to do that.'

Ginny froze, his use of the term 'honey' inexplicably triggering something in her. Despite the unsteadiness in his speech, there had seemed to her an almost impersonal slickness in his use of that casual endearment.

Her eyes dropped to the opened front of her dress, the memory of the look of triumph that had flickered across his face searing through her as she hastily drew the torn edges of her bra over her exposed breasts and rebuttoned the dress.

'Come on—let's get home,' he called to her, as he returned to the car and got in.

Ginny followed unsteadily, trying desperately to bring a semblance of order to the turmoil of her mind as she opened the passenger door.

'I'm meeting someone,' she stated, and was filled with disbelief at the toneless calmness she had managed to inject into the lie.

She stood by the open door, the thought drifting through her mind that she was in danger of becoming a total stranger to herself.

'OK—you're meeting someone,' he muttered brusquely. 'So get in.'

Ginny did so, the acute tension in her suddenly giving way to an uncontrollable shaking that made it impossible for her to do up her seatbelt.

Not a word was uttered between them when he removed the belt from her fumbling hands and clicked it into place. And neither was a single word uttered by either of them when he reached out and curved his hand against the nape of her neck and turned her head to his.

There was a numbingly bruising harshness in the

kiss he gave her before abruptly releasing her and starting up the car.

'Better not be late,' he said, the drawled words almost drowned by the protesting screech of tyres as he slammed down his foot and swung the car back on to the road.

The drive to the tiny village, a scant couple of kilometres off the coast road, passed in a blur to Ginny as she battled to rid herself of the mind-blowing violence of need which still kept welling up in her and washing over her in huge, uncontrollable waves. It wasn't that she was abnormal, she told herself numbly, it was simply that sexual awakening had come to her somewhat later than usual—and little wonder, with her repressed background. There had been a part of her that had craved to experience desire—if only to convince herself that she hadn't been tainted, not by her one clumsy experience, but by her aunt's abnormally prudish attitude to sex. But she had never envisaged those feelings being awoken in her by a man she thoroughly disliked most of the time, she thought with a small shiver of horror, nor the effect their devastating intensity would have on her. . . She could analyse it all till she was blue in the face, she told herself despondently, but it wasn't going to change anything.

'There's an eating place down there,' he stated, slowing the powerful car by the entrance to a narrow side-street.

'Yes, that's it,' muttered Ginny, her only wish to escape the suffocating atmosphere as soon as she could.

'You're sure of this?'

'Of course I'm sure,' she exclaimed, the pitch of her voice rising with tension.

'What time shall I pick you up?' he asked, drawing the car to a halt outside a rather dingy-looking restaurant.

'That won't be necessary, thank you,' replied Ginny stiffly, her hands once more fumbling with the seatbelt. 'I can get a lift back.' She gritted her teeth as long, lean fingers completed what her own were finding such a task, then gave a sharp moan of protest when her hands became trapped in his. 'Stop this, Michael!' she exploded, violently twisting her hands in her efforts to free them. 'Just stop it!'

'Stop what, Ginny?' he enquired with infuriating innocence.

'I don't know!' she choked. 'Just stop it!'

'Ginny, just because you feel guilty going to meet another guy when you'd rather be with me, you—'

'Just leave me alone!' she flung at him, close to breaking point. 'And stop trying to manipulate me!'

'I don't want you spending the evening with another guy—that's not being manipulative, it's being honest!'

'Honest?' she howled, then made an all-out effort to pull herself together. 'Michael, you and I are chalk and cheese, so it's hardly surprising I find your sudden switch to amorousness a trifle unconvincing!'

'A trifle unconvincing?' he enquired, in that infuriating parody of an English accent he now and then adopted. 'Has no one ever told you about the attraction of opposites? Very exciting, as I think you'll admit we're both discovering. . .and potentially also very dangerous.' He released her hands and switched on the interior light of the car. 'Don't you have a purse with you?'

'A purse?' queried Ginny bemusedly, in the instant before her heart landed in the vicinity of her stomach.

She had placed her bag on the hall table, ready to pick up as she left. . .

'I meant a bag—the thing you keep a comb and lipstick in,' he explained. 'You look a mess.'

Ginny dragged her fingers half-heartedly through her hair; this was a nightmare to end all nightmares, she told herself distractedly.

'You missed a bit,' he murmured, reaching out and ruffling his fingers lightly through her hair. 'And do you always do your dress up that way?'

Ginny's eyes flew to the front of her dress, humiliation burning through her when she discovered she had missed out a button.

'Shall I do it for you?'

'I can manage perfectly well myself,' she hissed, viciously slapping aside the tanned hand reaching out to her.

'That's better,' he murmured when she had finished, catching her chin in his hand. 'But there's nothing that can be done about your mouth.' He leaned over and kissed her with the same bruising swiftness he had when they had re-entered the car. 'It still looks as though you've just been thoroughly made love to—too bad you haven't, eh, Ginny? And too bad for the guy who might have spent all evening wondering if you had.'

She reached out to open the door, then dropped her head against the coolness of the window as a harsh sob choked from her.

'Don't worry, Ginny, he's not going to have the chance to wonder,' he muttered thickly, starting up the car. 'Because there's no way I would ever have let you walk into a dive like that.'

'You. . . I. . . So what was all this charade about

tidying me up?' she demanded furiously, while inwardly swooning with relief. 'Why did you—?'

'I was calling your bluff,' he cut in harshly. 'Hell, a dive like—'

'What do you mean—a dive?' she demanded, determined to fight to the last rather than betray one iota of her colossal relief. 'Not everyone's rolling in money the way you are. Some of us—'

'For God's sake, Ginny, can't you. . .? Oh, to hell with this! Do up your belt!'

They were back on the coast road before Ginny's fumbling fingers finally succeeded in carrying out that bellowed order, but even by then, her niggling feelings of humiliation and anger were still not encroaching with any significance on the magnitude of her relief.

CHAPTER FOUR

NOT a word was exchanged between them on the journey back to the villa, though Ginny felt no inclination whatever to interrupt the charged silence between them. But it was a silence she was finding all too depressingly familiar—the type to which she had been subjected far too often by her aunt ever to mistake the self-righteous recrimination it exuded.

She found herself recoiling sharply from the idea of comparing Michael's behaviour with that of her aunt. It was something she kept doing and, whatever his faults, it was unfair, she told herself vehemently, and was immediately disconcerted by the strength of her vehemence.

It was just that these past few months in France had brought it home to her just how fraught and negative and totally lacking in any sense of peace all those years with her aunt had been, she thought despondently, and now Michael had turned up and changed her peaceful haven into this terrible nightmare. . . But that still didn't give her any right to compare him with her aunt.

Confused by and resentful of the element of protectiveness towards him that had crept into her thoughts, Ginny occupied her mind for the rest of the journey back by counting telegraph-poles.

When they arrived, she leapt from the car and, once inside the house, made for the staircase with the intention of going straight to her room. She didn't care what he thought—she had had enough for tonight.

The sudden grasp of fingers on her arm halted her flight.

'And where do you think you're going?'

'It's not a question of *thinking*—I'm *going* to my room.'

Her captured arm was yanked from her side, carrying her with it in the wake of the man striding towards the kitchen.

'Why stand on ceremony?' she demanded, incensed. 'Why not just grab me by the hair?'

'Because I'm managing fine like this,' he replied, halting her by a chair. 'Sit down.'

'Just who do you think——?'

He placed both hands on her shoulders and pressed—Ginny sat.

'I suppose you just happen to keep a rope on you,' she flung at him, while her mind, as though to appease her mounting anger, sneaked a look what might have happened had he not so high-handedly brought her back and, more to the point, at what stage her complete lack of money would actually have dawned on her. It was a thought that sent a shudder through her, which in turn brought a visible start from the man towering over her.

'Would you like coffee?' he asked abruptly, walking over to the counter.

'No,' she muttered, thrown off guard by the unexpectedness both of his action and offer. 'On second thoughts—yes, I would,' she vacillated, surprising herself probably more than she did him. 'I'll make it.'

'No—I'll do it. I need something to occupy my hands,' he retorted brusquely.

'So do I.'

He spun round to face her, the fury in his expression knocking the breath from her.

'But mine could do so much more harm than yours ever could,' he informed her with steely venom. 'And just what the hell have you to be mad about, anyway?'

Ginny's mouth was dry and her heart racing. He had started when she had flinched, and had immediately walked away from her. It had crossed her mind he had done so because he had misinterpreted her involuntary shudder as one of fear. . . But now, just a few seconds later, she was experiencing actual physical fear and doing so for the first time in her life.

'If you're trying to frighten me—you've succeeded,' she stated shakily, and immediately questioned the wisdom of such a statement to a man who was quite obviously unbalanced—she had been so acutely aware of every other facet of him, so how had she possibly missed this most disturbing of ones?

'What do you mean—if I'm trying to frighten you?' he exclaimed, shock diluting the fury on his face. 'Why the hell would I try to frighten you?'

'I've no idea,' retorted Ginny, the genuineness of his reaction blunting the edge of her fear, 'but when a man of your size and obvious strength talks about needing to occupy his hands——'

'For God's sake, are you clean out of your mind?' he exploded, dragging his hands in disbelief through his hair. 'I didn't mean. . . Darn it, do you always take what's said to you in anger so literally?'

'How else am I supposed to take it?'

He swung back towards the sink, filling a pan with water, then putting it on the cooker to boil.

'Faults I may have aplenty, but violence is not one of them,' he eventually responded, the difficulty he was having containing his anger palpable, 'and even my no-longer-adoring niece will back me on that one. If you hadn't made me so angry——'

'Exactly what am I supposed to have done to make you so angry?' demanded Ginny indignantly, her fears for her physical safety forgotten as those for his mental stability increased.

'I'm not sure and that's what makes me so mad,' he retorted, his words doing nothing to reassure her. 'And that's something you and I are going to clear up right now.'

The instant Ginny rose to her feet, he spun round, the boiling water in the pan he had just lifted splashing up his arm.

'You're not leaving here until——'

'I'm getting cups, for heaven's sake,' said Ginny, trying her hardest to ignore the voice inside her telling her she was alone in this house with a probable madman.

'Right,' he said, when they were both seated at the table, their coffee poured. 'Who were you meeting tonight?'

'I really don't think that's any of your business,' retorted Ginny—to the horror of the inner voice that immediately told her she should be humouring him.

His mouth tightened to a harsh line of anger.

'OK,' he said, with a shrug that didn't for one moment fool her. 'What's that place like? I assume you've been there before.'

'It's cheap and cheerful, but Libby and I like it a lot,' replied Ginny, trying her hardest to sound natural, while mentally crossing her fingers. No matter how cheap or cheerful a place, the budget she and Libby existed on didn't run to eating out. 'Though obviously it's not the sort of place that someone like you would choose to go to.'

'What makes you say that, Ginny?' he asked, the

words almost conversational, the eyes above the mouth that uttered them glittering ice.

'Just one look at the place brought forth derogatory remarks from you.'

'I'm not a man to judge a book by its cover,' he muttered, then continued, 'So—you and Libby go there regularly, is that what you're telling me?'

'No, we. . .' Ginny hesitated, the feeling that she was somehow being led into a trap suddenly looming in her. 'We might have been there a couple of times.'

'And they were good times?'

'I. . . Look, why are you asking all these questions?' she stammered, certain that whatever the trap was, she was now well and truly in it.

'OK, Ginny, if you want it straight, why did you make up this story about having to meet someone tonight?'

'Are you calling me a—?'

'A liar? Yes, I damn well am!'

'Oh, I see—so any woman who passes up the chance of an evening in your delightful company, simply because she has something else arranged, has to be not only a raving nut-case, but also a liar!' she retaliated hotly.

'Let's just say that only a raving nut-case would so bare-facedly admit to frequenting the local pick-up joint.'

'I. . . You. . .' floundered Ginny, her eyes wide with shocked disbelief. 'Don't be so ridiculous—the local people would never tolerate such a—'

'They don't have much choice—it's been in existence so long it's part of local folklore.'

Ginny picked up her cup and drank from it, the discomfort its scalding contents caused her an almost welcome distraction from the hot waves of mortification washing over her—this just wasn't fair!

'So, let's start again, shall we?' he murmured, settling back comfortably on his chair. 'Why did you lie to me?'

'I'd have thought that was pretty obvious,' retorted Ginny, her mind having scrabbled in search of a credible variation on her story for only one frantic instant before giving up.

'If it was obvious, I'd not be asking you.'

'I didn't wish to spend an evening in your company.'

'So why didn't you just come out and say so?'

'I probably would have with any normal person,' retorted Ginny. 'I just found it easier to lie than leave myself open to another bout of your browbeating tactics.'

'You just find it easier to lie—period,' he stated coldly. 'The last thing I'm likely to do is start browbeating, as you put it, a woman I've just asked out as a gesture of apology.' He took an orange from the fruit bowl on the table and started peeling it.

'If you're hungry,' exclaimed Ginny, clutching at the only straw presenting itself, 'I'll cook you something.'

'Stay where you are,' he snapped as she made to rise. 'This will do me fine,' he added, his eyes darkly brooding as they watched her. 'That Frenchman Libby got herself involved with,' he continued unexpectedly, his tone switching to conversational, 'is he still on the scene?'

'Would it bother you if he was?' was Ginny's surprised and involuntary retort.

'Is she in love with him?'

'I didn't even say he was still on the scene,' protested Ginny, before angrily telling herself there was nothing to protest about—what business of his was it, anyway?

'Well, if he is, he sounds bad news,' muttered Michael, frowning. 'Though I was intrigued to hear that he was working on an oil rig. . . Not quite in keeping with his playboy reputation, but there again, his folks might have something to do with that, as they own the rig in question.'

'What am I supposed to do, congratulate you on the thoroughness of your bloodhounds?' demanded Ginny through clenched teech. 'I'm afraid they're going to find investigating me terribly dull,' she added, experiencing a twinge of guilt as she found herself thinking how much easier life would be for her if they had discovered Libby's condition.

'We'll find out soon enough,' he murmured, with no hint of discomfiture at so bizarre an admission.

Ginny flashed him a look of disgust. 'The terrible thing is that you actually regard it as normal—investigating people at the drop of a hat.'

'No—never at the drop of a hat,' he informed her grimly, 'not even in business. I thought long and hard before I had this de Montoussé guy Libby was involved with checked.'

'Oh, yes,' exclaimed Ginny sceptically, 'and you agonised for weeks over putting your bloodhounds on me!'

'You just don't get it, do you, Ginny?' he murmured ironically. 'I didn't come down here with my mind filled with suspicion and set on giving Libby the third degree. OK, so I kept a few loose tabs on her—with her history, I'd have been crazy not to—but as far as I knew she'd been in no trouble since arriving in France, and I was prepared to believe what you keep telling me is a fact, that she had at last grown up. All I wanted was for us to be on good terms again—I even tried calling here a couple of times to let her know I was coming, but I didn't get any reply. Then I met you, Ginny.' He gave a bitter laugh. 'If you'd had a placard slung round your neck with "guilty" emblazoned on it, you couldn't have aroused any more suspicion in me than you managed to just about every time you opened your mouth. So no, I didn't have to think hard about having you checked.'

'Don't you dare try to justify your police-state mentality by making such ridiculous claims about me,' Ginny rounded on him, devastated to find that, far from finding his claims ridiculous, she could easily believe them.

'OK, I have a police-state mentality and I make ridiculous claims about you,' he said, his words accompanied by a chillingly mirthless laugh. 'I guess only a mind like mine would find in any way strange your earlier zero reaction to my telling you Libby had called. I guess only a mind as low as mine would put you to the test as I did just now. . . And, guess what—you failed.'

'Surprise, surprise,' muttered Ginny, her blood running cold at the idea of having, yet again, blindly leapt into another of his traps. 'So what have I done wrong this time?' she demanded, straightening her shoulders as she tried to summon up the will to get up and leave. The instant she moved, her entire body tensed in shock as the torn edges of her bra, disturbed by that slight movement, grazed erotically against her flesh.

He laughed, a soft, groaning laugh that made Ginny suspect for one crazy, panic-stricken moment that he knew what was happening to her.

'Oh, Ginny, sometimes you manage to sound——' He broke off with an impatient toss of his head, the laughter fading from his features. 'What you did wrong this time was to duck and weave, when I started asking you questions about Libby just now, instead of pointing out I could ask her all the questions I wanted myself in a couple of days.'

He glanced over at her, his expression quizzical.

'I'm sorry,' muttered Ginny, almost afraid to move for fear of the devastating effect those couple of torn scraps of material might wreak once more on her body. 'But if my mind worked as tortuously as yours appears to, I'd consider I had a problem.'

'You make it sound as though you don't consider you have one,' he murmured easily, 'but you do. You and I have this one rather major problem in common.'

'You're right,' stated Ginny, rising to her feet and almost reeling at the mind-blowing memory of the feel of his hands against her flesh as she did so. 'And that problem is you and your over-active imagination.'

'Now, that really wasn't very bright of you,' said Michael, genuine amusement softening his face as he also rose. 'You shouldn't make statements that can be so easily disproved,' he added, strolling over to her and chuckling softly as he gazed down at her.

'We'll see,' retorted Ginny, the hot, stomach-churning effect of his laughter sending a welter of mind-numbing questions scurrying through her head. 'I'll be quite happy to accept your apology when you've been proved wrong.'

He started to say something that ended up lost in laughter. Mesmerised, Ginny gazed up at him, the throbbing heat searing through her tempered by a sudden sadness. Had her life been normal, this was precisely the sort of man on whom she should have been having crushes during her teenage years—instead of, at twenty-three, being worried sick that she was falling in love with him.

'We can settle just how over-active this imagination

of mine is or isn't right now,' he said, once he had sufficiently recovered, and took her in his arms.

Their mouths met in a mutual surge of hunger while their bodies, as though by common consent, picked up where they had left off in the moonlight less than two hours before.

'Ginny, this is crazy,' he muttered thickly, his lips devouring hers while his hands moved confidently against the contours of her body, sending buttons scattering as they impatiently reached inside her dress to cup the breasts straining for his touch.

'Of course it's crazy,' she gasped, a dizzying, exhilarating sense of liberation sweeping gloriously through her—worrying never stopped anything happening, so why worry?

Her arms reached up to him, her fingers entwining themselves feverishly in the luxuriant thickness of his hair, while her body, charged almost beyond endurance by the maddening touch of his hands, moulded itself in uninhibited invitation to the harsh contours of his.

'So crazy that if we had any sense we'd stop right now,' he protested hoarsely, the hotness of his mouth against hers denying his words, as did the hands that roamed restlessly against her trembling body. 'Ginny, we could both regret it if we don't stop now,' he groaned, the words driven from him on a jagged breath.

Wordlessly she shook her head, a crystal-clear core within the chaotic tumult of sensation racking her telling her that, way beyond the physical need engulfing her, there was a deeper need in her to be fulfilled, and that no regret would ever compare with that of denying that undefined need.

He swung her up in his arms and carried her through

the doorway and out into the hallway and up the stairs. She lay in his arms, her face pressed against the hollow of his neck, her body close to being overwhelmed by the sensations bombarding it, her mind alive and noting with a curiously analytical delight the feather-light kisses landing here and there on her head. With each step he took and with each kiss that landed, that undefined need within her grew more and more insistent. When they reached the darkened landing, she reached out and turned on the light, placing her hand against his cheek and turning his head towards her as she raised her own to gaze up at him.

He paused momentarily, the breath catching harshly in his throat as the bewitching darkness in his eyes hotly caressed hers, before striding on towards his room. He stopped at the open doorway, his eyes still locked with hers as he lowered her slowly to her feet.

He reached up, his hands capturing hers and gently removing her arms from around his neck.

'It's still not too late,' he said, his words hoarse and distorted with strain.

But it was too late, she suddenly understood with completely clarity. Her only chance to escape loving him had been to leave the day he had arrived—all that worrying had made no difference and now it was far, far too late.

'Ginny, please,' he begged huskily, his hands tightening compulsively around hers.

'It's not too late for you either,' she whispered unsteadily, the burning darkness in his eyes fanning the fire of the need raging within her.

'It was too late for me the moment I——' He broke off with a harsh groan and pulled her into his arms. 'Ginny, I want you too much to be able to think clearly,' he muttered indistinctly against her hair. 'It's all so crazy—I didn't come here to hound Libby, yet——'

'Michael, there's nothing for you to worry about where Libby's concerned, I promise you,' she whispered, love spilling over in her as she clung fiercely to him, searching for the words that would help him understand without betraying her friend. 'It's just that——'

'No!' he protested, his mouth silencing hers with an impassioned kiss. 'You've said all I needed to hear.'

His arms released her, but his eyes continued to hold her, gathering her to him in the smouldering heat of a caress that sent a shudder of longing coursing through her.

When he took her hand in his and led her through the doorway, she followed him in trance-like silence.

Her need to be back in his arms overwhelming, she turned to him, her arms rising towards him. But he stepped back from her, then reached out and began slowly undoing the remaining buttons of her dress.

Apprehension stirring in her, Ginny glanced up, only to find his eyes lowered from hers, trained on the fingers meticulously performing their task.

She hadn't wanted to love him—wouldn't have chosen to had she had the choice, she thought distractedly as her apprehension began to give way to panic. She wanted him with a desperation she had never dreamed capable of, but his wanting her had nothing to do with love.

Her breath catching in her throat, she gazed down at those slim fingers, so tanned aginst the paleness of her dress, and felt love swell like a fierce pain within her as the tremor, so plainly visible in those hands, told her far more than any words ever could.

Slowly and with infinite gentleness, those elegant

long fingers painstakingly undid the buttons running the length of her dress.

'Michael,' she gasped, the need to feel his arms around her more than she could bear.

He silenced her with the swift hunger of his kiss, kicking his feet free of his shoes while his hands slid her dress from around her.

His mouth still on hers, he impatiently tore off his shirt; but still he didn't take her in his arms.

'Michael,' she begged, reaching out to him.

She heard his sharp intake of breath as her fingers curled against the matted darkness of his chest, and her own soft cry of pleasure as her fingers spread and the impatience of his need was revealed by the heavy pounding of his heart beneath her hands.

Yet even when he placed his hands on her shoulders, it wasn't to hold her, but to ease aside the straps of her torn bra. Then he drew it down her arms, forcing her hands to break their contact with the pounding beat of his heart as he removed it completely.

'Why won't you hold me?' she demanded with the boldness of sheer frustration, flinging herself against him.

His answer was a groaned shiver of laughter, but his arms encircled her, his hands sliding impatiently against the silken softness of her skin as though preparing to explore its every pore.

'I was afraid of rushing you,' he whispered against her hair. 'And—and of losing my head the moment I had you in my arms.'

'I don't mind if you lose your head,' she protested, before becoming irretrievably lost in the shivering caress of his answering laughter and the wonderment of what was happening to her.

As though suddenly freed, his hands and mouth

were laying ardent siege to every part of her body. She felt a taut, erotic heat swell in her breasts as they were crushed against the tingling abrasiveness of his chest-hairs, and she resisted fiercely when she felt him draw back slightly from her, reluctant to be so soon deprived of such sensuous contact. But then, while his mouth searched hotly against her throat, his hands became instruments of an exquisite, caressing torture, dragging an explosive cry of pleasure from her as they played in maddening gentleness against her turgid breasts.

She pleaded in brief protest when those hands moved away and down to the curve of her waist, but her protest turned once again to pleasure when the hot search of his mouth on her breasts replaced the hands now sliding down her body and taking with them the silky triangle of her briefs as they caressed the golden length of her legs.

She kicked off her shoes as he swung her back up into his arms and carried her to the bed.

'Ginny,' he murmured, her name almost a question on his lips as he began lowering her on to the bed. He hesitated for a fraction of a moment, the burning promise in the eyes seeking and holding hers sending involuntary shudders of longing jarring through her. 'It's just us now, Ginny,' he whispered fiercely, his mouth seeking hers in a groan of hunger as his arms released her. 'Us and no one else.'

She clung to him, her lips making their own explicit demands, her refusal to be parted from him for even the briefest of instants severely hampering his movements as he shed the rest of his clothing.

Her body welcomed his with shameless abandon when he at last joined her, her arms restless and impatient as they encircled his neck, her legs almost predatory as they entwined themselves in the muscled length of his, her every sense revelling drunkenly in the desire so urgently manifesting itself in the powerful body to which her own so uninhibitedly clung.

'Michael!' she choked in desperation, fighting off his attempts to curb the impatient urgency spilling over in her. 'I. . . There's no danger of you rushing me!'

'Is there not?' he whispered, laughter rippling through him.

'Not in the least!'

His lips silencing her protests, he reached over to the drawer of the bedside table, his kiss a bruising testament to the hunger within him as his legs tensed and freed themselves from hers. When he eased himself slightly from her, his mouth still imposing its bruising silence on hers, her hands softly explored the contours of his back, a sudden shyness in her overriding the yearning in her to help him or even to acknowledge what he was doing.

Then his mouth released hers and she could sense the almost unbearable tension beneath the sudden stillness in him as his hands began moving in a gentle, yet mind-blowingly intimate exploration of her body that finally brought an involuntary gasp of startled pleasure from her.

'I guess you're right,' he whispered, his voice far from steady. 'There isn't the least danger of your being rushed.'

Injudicious though her one and only previous experience of lovemaking had been, there had been nothing in those tenderly clumsy fumblings to scar her either physically or mentally, though, as she had matured, her apparent lack of sexual appetite had now and then made her fret that she might indeed have been somehow scarred. But that one experience had left her in no way prepared: not for the explosive force of the unleashed desire invading her body; not for her own body's unequivocal welcome of so potent an invasion; and most certainly not for those tight buds of pulsating excitement that began erupting without warning deep within her. One moment she was revelling in the wonderment of what was happening to her, the next she was gasping out his name in shock as one by one those buds blossomed into shattering explosions of pleasure. Later, when that cycle had begun repeating itself with an almost excruciating intensity, his name had deteriorated on her lips to a soft, incoherent moan. And later still, when she felt she was on the verge of recognising a pattern in the innumerable pleasures erupting within her, the soft, breathless words he cried out to her and the increased urgency in the thrusting rhythm of his powerful body changed everything. Sensation after exquisite sensation began dancing back and forth between their locked bodies; rampaging sensations that swelled and multiplied out of all control until they finally merged into one devastating explosion that ripped between them, tearing the breath from their lungs and almost the life from their bodies.

Locked in near-comatose breathlessness in one another's arms, it was several minutes before either was capable of speech.

'No!' protested Ginny, when Michael at last made to move from her.

'I'm not going anywhere,' he promised hoarsely, then added with a breathlessly distorted chuckle of disbelief, 'I'm not *capable* of going anywhere right now.'

Ginny's heart was turning somersaults of contentment as he settled himself on his back and gathered her against him—that note of disbelief in his words had only confirmed what her every instinct had already told her.

'Ginny,' he murmured, his fingers ruffling lazily in her hair.

'Mmm?'

'Nothing—just Ginny.'

'I can't think of what to say either,' she gulped breathlessly, and felt tears prickling inexplicably in her eyes as she pressed her cheek against the moist heat of his skin and breathed in the subtle, intoxicatingly masculine scent of him. 'It's just that. . .I had no idea.' She hesitated, searching for words that refused to come. 'I had no idea it would be like that.'

'You what?' he exclaimed, rising on to an elbow and peering down at her. 'Damn—I can't see you properly,' he muttered, reaching over and switching on a bedside light.

'Michael—it's so bright!' she protested, burying her face against him.

He angled the light away from them and drew her face from him.

'Ginny, are you saying you'd never made love before?' he demanded, his eyes troubled.

'No, I. . . Of course I wasn't,' she responded irritably, annoyed that he had disturbed the beautifully hazy bliss enveloping her. 'I was eighteen when I lost my virginity,' she added, remembering the innumerable times her aunt had warned her that no 'decent' man would want anything to do with her once he knew that terrible fact.

'Eighteen?' he echoed, but his eyes had lost none of their luminous softness as he gazed down at her, even though they had widened slightly.

'Are you shocked?' she asked, a residual part of

her, she was horrified to discover, still apprehensive that her aunt's dire predictions could come true.

'Shocked?' he murmured, dropping a kiss on to the end of her nose before returning to a prone position. 'Ginny, what possible right would I have to be shocked?'

His words hit her with the force of a blow, yet she knew instantly that her reaction was completely irrational. There was the look in his eyes, that casual little kiss he had just given her, and the fact that he had drawn her even more firmly into his arms as he lay back down, she listed almost obsessively to herself. But the blissful haze had now deserted her completely. Had he admitted to being shocked, she would have been horrified, she remonstrated angrily with herself—unlike her aunt, who lived in some sort of medieval time-warp. Even the law considered someone of eighteen a fully fledged adult! But however much she reasoned with herself, all she saw in his words was the stark reminder that the all-consuming love she felt for him was in no way reciprocated.

'It's funny,' he murmured, the softness of his words piercing through the bleakness of her thoughts, 'but I have difficulty picturing you as a woman at eighteen. . . I guess that's because you often don't look much more than fifteen when you're pottering around the garden in your dungarees.'

And she hadn't been the most mature of eighteen-year-olds, thought Ginny, bitterly regretting ever having mentioned the fact. 'I wasn't exactly sophistication personified at eighteen, if that's what you mean.'

'Hey, Ginny,' he admonished softly, his hand stroking placatingly against her shoulder. 'Why so prickly? I'm not making any judgements. It's not as though you were a juvenile—and the guy must have been pretty special——'

'Of course he was special,' burst out Ginny. 'Next to Libby he was the best friend I ever had!'

'Friend?'

'Yes, I. . . Unfortunately we both discovered that friendship isn't necessarily a good basis for sex.'

'So how come you tried it?'

'Because. . . I suppose because we were both lonely and unhappy. His parents had just separated and he was going to live with his mother somewhere hundreds of miles away and. . .' Her words faltered to a halt as he hugged her tightly to him.

'Let me guess,' he murmured indistinctly against her hair. 'You were the sort of kid who always brought stray and injured animals home.'

'I probably would have been, but my aunt wouldn't allow pets over her threshold.'

'Your aunt?'

'My mother's much older sister—I had to live with her after my parents were killed in a car crash.'

'How old were you?'

'Ten.'

His arms tightened around her and he pressed his lips against her forehead, letting them linger there in wordless comfort. But far from being comforted by his tender concern, she found herself filling with an aching sense of loss. She had never had his love to lose in the first place, she reminded herself brutally, and whatever tenderness he might be feeling towards her had a lot to do with the aftermath of what they had just shared and nothing to do with love.

'This first lover of yours—how did you meet him?'

'His family moved next door—just after Libby left. He was also in my class.'

'And did you keep in touch with him once he'd left?'

Ginny shook her head. 'We lost touch completely. You see, my aunt found out what had happened and all hell was let loose——'

'You were eighteen, for heaven's sake.'

'If I'd been twelve or thirty, it wouldn't have made any difference to my aunt. He wrote letter after letter, and each time one would arrive she would wave it unopened in front of me, then tear it up. . . Eventually they stopped coming.'

'Ginny, I'm sorry,' he groaned, hugging her tightly to him. 'It must have been hell for you. . .but at least you managed to come out of it without any sexual hang-ups, though God only knows how.'

She turned in his arms and lay with her back to him, resenting his words and shaken by the intensity of the physical need suddenly burgeoning in her despite that resentment.

'As far as my aunt was concerned, I'd become the archetypal fallen woman—there for the taking of any man who so much as looked at me. But you and she couldn't be more wrong—until tonight, that first time was the only time.'

She felt the sudden tension that shot through him, stilling even his breathing, and was glad. He plainly didn't like being lumped together with her aunt—well, tough, because neither did she like loving and needing him the way she did, and a desperate part of her wanted to drive him away before this terrible need for him took control of her.

'Ginny. . . I don't know what to say,' he muttered eventually, his words hoarse with shock.

'You don't have to say anything,' she responded tonelessly, and sat up.

'Don't go.'

'You haven't eaten—you must be hungry.'

'Are you hungry?'

She turned her face away, afraid he would see the hunger in her that had nothing to do with food.

He drew her back down into his arms, the need in him as ravenous as hers.

CHAPTER FIVE

GINNY'S progression from sleep to wakefulness was slow: first a vague, sensuous lethargy caressing her body, next the stirrings of memories that belonged to the realm of dreams. Then her eyes opened and she saw him, the man who had become precisely what she had frivolously dubbed him at first sight—the man of her dreams, her lover.

He was standing at the foot of the bed, dressed in lightweight trousers and a dark, short-sleeved shirt. He was looking down the length of the bed and straight into her newly awakened eyes, but his eyes were no longer those of the lover whose uninhibited passion had ignited a response in her from which her body still ached; they were the coldly guarded eyes of a stranger and they filled her with a terrible foreboding.

'Good morning,' he said, his greeting formal yet wary.

'Is it?' she asked, apprehension rendering her incapable of any pretence. 'A good morning, I mean,' she expanded hoarsely.

'If you want to pick a fight, Ginny,' he drawled, 'that's OK by me.'

'Pick a fight with you?' she whispered dazedly, their recently shared passion still too vibrant a force in her for the brutality of his coldness to penetrate fully.

'What did you expect—that I'd be eating out of your hand?' he demanded, his veneer of coldness slipping momentarily to reveal a rage that at last got through to her.

'Michael, stop it!' she gasped, horror-stricken. 'If you regret last night—say so! Don't. . .' Her words were drowned by the raucous harshness of his laughter as he strode round to the side of the bed and sat down on it.

'Do you regret last night?' he demanded, catching her by the arms and pulling her against him.

'Michael, I——'

This time it was the sharp hunger of his kiss that halted her words and deleted all thought from her mind as she responded with a spontaneous intensity that made mockery of his question. But when she made to put her arms around him, he drew back, shaking his head vehemently. For several seconds his eyes burned angrily down into hers, then he rose and returned to the foot of the bed.

'Don't think that I wouldn't love to spend the rest of the day in your arms,' he murmured with patent insincerity, his gaze switching to one of blank remoteness, 'but I shan't be around much today—I have business to attend to.'

Ginny watched in stunned silence as he began walking towards the door, part of her still unable to comprehend that any of this could really be happening. . . But it was happening, all right, she told herself with growing disgust, and to think that she actually loved a man who could behave like this!

'Oh, by the way—Libby called,' he stated, halting and turning by the door. 'Big surprise—she won't be able to make it here tomorrow after all,' he added, venom seeping into his words despite the palpable control he was exercising over himself. 'Though I guess the only surprise for you would have been if she'd showed up.'

So that was what this was all about, she thought

numbly, hopelessness encompassing her like a suffocating cloud.

'Michael, why couldn't you have told me this right away, instead of—?'

'And why couldn't you have told me, instead of lying in your teeth the way you did?' he snarled.

'Michael, I—'

'Michael, I *promise* you,' he parodied savagely, 'you have *nothing* to worry about where Libby's concerned—'

'And you *haven't*!' howled Ginny distractedly.

'OK,' he challenged softly, 'tell me you believed she'd be coming tomorrow.'

'I—I can't,' she whispered defeatedly. 'But that still doesn't mean you have anything to worry about—'

'Spare me the speech, honey, I've already heard it several times before,' he drawled. 'Like I said, I've things to do today. . . Which reminds me, I shall be bringing one of the company's accountants back here—and also, the woman the agents were to contact about doing the laundry is due today, so have her prepare one of the guest-rooms.'

Ginny sank back against the pillows as the door closed behind her, her mind frozen in horror. What had she expected—a miracle? That she would wake this morning and find herself bathed in the fairy-tale of Michael's love? She shook her head vehemently. She wasn't a complete fool, but she certainly hadn't expected anything like this. And the terrible thing was that she couldn't really blame him for his suspicions about Libby, she reasoned numbly, tears pricking hotly against her eyes; she couldn't even blame Libby for landing her in this soul-destroying nightmare, because Libby had warned her right from the start. She had no one to blame but herself, she concluded bitterly, then leapt from the bed and raced to the shower.

It was only when she had scrubbed her body almost raw that the pain inside her began turning to anger. Never once, during all the hours of puritanical ranting to which her aunt had subjected her, had she ever doubted her own integrity, she thought with a savage bitterness. Yet, within moments of her awaking, this man she loved and to whom she had last night given herself in nothing but love, had managed to make her feel tainted—so unclean that she was reduced to this pathetic, ritualised scrubbing!

Galvanised by helpless rage into a bout of hyperactivity, she forced herself to strip the bed in which she had made the greatest mistake in her life, and then went to her room and stripped that bed too. She had remade both beds and made up another in one of the guest-rooms, and was sorting the laundry in the white-washed utility room, when the rap on the front door knocker brought her dervish-like racing around to a halt.

The woman the agents had sent, Madame Auberge, was slim and cheery and middle-aged; not only did she speak English far better than Ginny's French, but she had also worked at the villa on and off for several years.

It was only when Ginny took herself off into the garden, still in the grip of a fevered need to remain constantly occupied, that she noticed the oppressive humidity in the atmosphere. She sat back on her heels and was gazing up at the unfamiliar sight of a leaden, threatening sky when her attention was caught by the appearance of a car in the drive—a large, opulently stately car whose windows were darkened against prying eyes.

'Oh, no,' she groaned softly to herself. 'This is all I need, a visitation from another member of the illustrious Grant tribe!'

She rose reluctantly to her feet as the gleaming car drew to a halt beside her and watched wooden-faced as a window slid noiselessly open. The fact that the man who addressed her spoke in rapid, fluent French brought her a measure of relief.

'I'm afraid I don't speak much French,' she apologised, and was searching around for words in French when she was addressed in faultless English.

'I have come to see Miss Collier—Libby. Is she in?'

'Libby?' exclaimed Ginny. 'No—she's not here. She's in Paris.'

'And how soon will she be back?'

'She won't. . . I mean, she's gone to visit friends,' gabbled Ginny, and knew precisely what Michael had meant about her having had guilt written all over her when he had first met her. 'What I meant was, she won't be back today—she'll be staying there for a while,' she corrected herself. 'I'm a friend of hers and I could give her a message, if you like.'

'I should like very much,' murmured the man, not bothering to disguise his apparent amusement.

To Ginny's consternation, he then stepped from his car—a man probably in his early fifties, of medium height and dressed with the languid elegance of the very rich.

'Bernard de Maupéou,' he murmured, the shrewd eyes in a tanned, rather haughty face taking discreet stock of Ginny as he reached out a hand to her.

'Ginny Price,' replied Ginny, irritated to find herself wondering if she shouldn't have dusted off the hand she had just placed in his.

'You're obviously wondering who on earth I can

be,' he stated. 'I am Jean-Claude de Montoussé's uncle—his mother is my sister. It appears that, in the not too distant future, I shall also be your friend's uncle. Are you acquainted with my nephew?'

Ginny shook her head, the unsettling realisation dawning on her that a confrontation with this upper-crust relative of Jean-Claude's would probably turn out to be only marginally less traumatic than one with another Grant. 'No, I'm afraid he'd been sent. . . I mean——'

'You meant sent away,' murmured the Frenchman drily. 'That may seem harsh to you, but Jean-Claude and, it would appear, your friend have quite a past to live down between them. My sister and her husband thought long and hard before asking what they did of them—they are, believe it or not, exceedingly fond of the girl.' He glanced around him, his entire demeanour managing to convey that he wasn't used to being kept hanging around in drives. 'Anyway, I'm sorry to have missed her, but I believe her uncle is down here at the moment. . .'

'He's staying here—yes,' replied Ginny, torn as to whether or not she should invite him in. If she didn't, she ran the risk of offending one of Libby's future in-laws; if she did. . .

'Good,' said the Frenchman, a note of impatience creeping into his tone. 'I'd like to see him.'

'I'm afraid he's not here either at the moment,' exclaimed Ginny, squirming with indecision.

'It seems I'm not having much luck today,' he stated, giving Ginny a decidedly disapproving look.

'No, I'm afraid you're not,' agreed Ginny, reluctantly accepting she had no choice. 'I can't think of anything worse than a wasted journey in weather as oppressive a this,' she added, 'so the least I can do is invite you in for refreshment—coffee, or perhaps something cold?'

'Something cold sounds most tempting,' murmured Bernard de Maupéou with a sigh. 'And as for this weather, I'm afraid it's the sort that makes me want to go straight back to Paris, where a storm is a storm and doesn't hang around for days, killing half the population, as it does here, while it decides whether or not to happen.'

Feeling awkward and wooden and most apprehensive, Ginny escorted him into the house, collected a large jug of iced lemonade from the kitchen and led him on into the conservatory—decidedly the coolest room in the house.

'I hadn't even noticed a storm was brewing until I went outside,' she said, having poured their drinks and feeling her duty to keep a semblance of conversation going, 'yet now I can feel it, even in here.'

The Frenchman nodded, then took a sip of his drink. 'This is very good,' he murmured appreciatively. 'So tell me how Libby's getting on with Jean-Claude banished.'

'She's missing him dreadfully, of course,' replied Ginny, feeling suddenly uncharacteristically resentful of her absent friend. All right, so the pregnancy was unplanned, but, according to Libby, she and Jean-Claude had intended starting a family straight away. . . It was ludicrous of her not to have let him know!

'As I'm sure he is missing her,' murmured Bernard de Maupéou, reaching in an inside pocket and bringing out a small notebook. 'If you give me her telephone number in Paris, I'll get my wife to give her a ring.'

Ginny's mouth went dry. 'I'm afraid I don't have it.'

'The name of the people with whom she's staying would do.'

'I've the most terrible head for names,' muttered Ginny, contorting her face into a frown of deep concentration before shaking her head. 'No—I'm sorry, it's gone completely,' she apologised.

'My, this *is* proving to be the most unproductive of visits,' observed the Frenchman drily, removing an engraved visiting card from the notebook and scribbling something on the back of it. 'Perhaps you could give this to Michael Grant—the number where I'm staying down here is on the back.'

Doing her best not to show her surprise that he should know Michael by name, Ginny took the card.

'I also have banking interests,' he explained obliquely. 'We've been putting out feelers to one another for some time now, but keep missing actually getting together. But perhaps that's something we could now get around to while we're both down here.' He rose. 'And if you could tell your friend Libby that I called and look forward to meeting her, I should be grateful.' He gave her an abruptly formal bow. 'It was most pleasant meeting you, Miss Price. . .and thank you once again for your hospitality.'

Ginny escorted him back to his car and, with a distinct feeling of unease, watched it disappear down the driveway. Another unmitigated disaster, she thought despondently. Perhaps she was over-reacting, but she had an uncomfortably strong feeling that it was only after she had been unable to come up with any means of contacting Libby that he had shown such interest in contacting Michael. He hadn't been inside five minutes, then suddenly he couldn't wait to leave. And as for his leave-taking, abrupt and chilly didn't begin to describe it. . . Yes, an unmitigated disaster, as had been her handling of just about every other aspect of this unwelcome subterfuge—but, to be perfectly honest, she was past caring.

After Madame Auberge had left, Ginny took her second shower of the day, standing under the freezing jets until her body was almost numb with cold.

Anger and desolation did battle within her, threatening to tear her apart, and it was only when anger once again got the upper hand that she was able to stir herself and go down to the kitchen.

The last thing she felt like doing was preparing a meal for a louse and one of his minions, she told herself savagely, opening the fridge door, then slamming it shut. And anyway, if he wanted her to cook for this accountant, he should have damned well asked her!

She clattered around the kitchen, generally letting off steam, but nearly jumped out of her skin when, having heard no sound of a car in the drive, she heard the front door open and the sound of voices in the hall.

Seconds later, Michael appeared in the kitchen.

'It's too hot to cook,' he stated, depositing several carrier-bags on the kitchen table. 'I picked up a few things from a *charcuterie* on the way back—we can have bread and salad with it.' He flopped down on a chair, his expression wan and slightly wary as he gazed up at her. 'Are you OK, Ginny? You look a bit——'

'You had a visitor today,' she interrupted coldly, unwilling to subject herself to any hypocritical concern on his part. 'A Bernard de Maupéou.'

'De Maupéou came round here?' he asked, puzzled.

Ginny dug in the pocket of her skirt and produced the visiting card—which she then placed on the table.

'He said that as you keep missing each other in Paris, perhaps you'd contact him on that number while he's here.' And he can tell you for himself whose uncle he is, she added mutinously to herself.

'Do you know who this guy is?' he asked quietly.

'He said he was a banker,' she replied, almost certain that wasn't what he meant: obviously his bloodhounds had done their work in that area.

'Yeah—he's a banker,' he drawled, then gave an angry shake of his head. 'Ginny, don't huff with me—we need to talk.'

'*You* may need to talk,' she informed him frigidly, 'but I have no desire whatever to do so. And, for your information, I'm not huffing with you.'

'Ginny, we can't pretend last night didn't happen,' he exclaimed impatiently.

'Perhaps not,' she rounded on him, driven by the aching void inside her, the effect his presence, the sound of his voice were having on her, 'but I'll happily give it a try!'

'Ginny, I didn't choose for things to be like this,' he protested wearily, reaching over and picking up the card she had placed on the table. 'Hell, all——' He broke off at the sound of high-heeled shoes tip-tapping in the distance. 'That'll be Aurelie Marais, the accountant I told you was coming,' he muttered, rising. 'Thank you for making up a room for her.'

'It's my job,' replied Ginny, and experienced a twinge of satisfaction at the expression of anger her words brought to his face before berating herself for being so pathetically childish.

Michael walked to the door as a small, slim woman of about Ginny's own age entered, and spoke rapidly to her in French.

'I'm afraid Aurelie speaks about as much English as you do French,' he informed Ginny once he had introduced them.

Aurelie Marais had a gusty, abandoned laugh and sharply twinkling eyes that were completely at odds with her almost ethereal good looks and the mass of Titian-coloured hair that frothed against her shoulders, and Ginny found herself warming to her instantly.

In fractured English, punctuated by bouts of laughter and several necessary interventions by Michael as a translator, Aurelie complained about the oppressiveness of the weather, downed two glasses of Ginny's lemonade and demanded the recipe, and offered to make a dressing for the salad Ginny had started preparing.

'I guess, as everyone's mucking in, I'd better do my bit,' murmured Michael, leaning against Ginny and reaching across her for a bowl of tomatoes.

Momentarily stunned by the effect that brief contact had had on her and by the erotic memories it instantly evoked in her, Ginny gazed sightlessly down at the lettuce she had just washed and gave silent thanks for Aurelie, who was still happily prattling on in her own private version of Franglais.

They ate early, mainly because Michael and Aurelie wanted to get a couple of hours' work done during the relative coolness of the evening. It was during the meal, taken in the coolness of the conservatory, rather than in the humid furnace the terrace still was, that Ginny found herself examining Aurelie, simply to keep her mind from Michael. The French girl's relationship with the American was relaxed and joky, amost flirtatious—yet something told Ginny that Aurelie's bubbly personality wouldn't always be regarded as a plus in the staid realms of accountancy and that she must be exceptionally good at her job to hold the position she did.

HOW TO PLAY
£ SIX HUNDRED THOUSAND
BIG BUCKS
AND YOU COULD WIN THE
£600,000
PLUS JACKPOT!
£ SIX HUNDRED THOUSAND
YOUR PERSONAL GAME CARD INSIDE...
Mills & Boon

'You're very quiet, Ginny,' observed Michael later, his eyes catching and holding hers.

'I'm afraid I'm pooped,' she muttered, dragging her eyes from his. 'I'll be glad when this storm breaks.'

'Pooped!' exclaimed Aurelie, pouncing on the word with delight. 'I am not pooped,' she laughed, rising. 'I shall make the coffee.'

When Michael made to get to his feet, the French girl placed her hands on his shoulder and forced him back down; when he made to speak, she cupped her hands over his mouth, winking over at Ginny and admonishing him softly in French as she leaned her torso against his head.

Ginny rose to her feet, forcing a smile to her lips and into her words. 'As you two have work to do and I'm too pooped even to think of coffee, I think I'll call it a day.'

'Call it a day?' queried Aurelie, so intrigued that she released her captive.

Ginny tried explaining in French, then gave up when Michael obligingly stepped in and bade her goodnight.

She went to her room, her mind resisting the thoughts it couldn't face as she prepared for bed and then flung herself down on it.

The weather wasn't helping, still and heavy and filled with foreboding, replicating the terrible pressure that had been building up in her all day. But she had broken before the weather showed any sign of doing so, something unleashing in her like a wild and vicious animal at the sight of Aurelie's casual display of intimacy towards Michael—jealousy: an emotion she had never before experienced and one that had shaken her to the core.

The sooner she got away from this place, the better, she told herself despairingly; she had had enough—

enough of feeling so thoroughly disorientated that she could barely distinguish up from down, and enough of this madness of kidding herself that this mindless, joyless, all-consuming torture she was undergoing was in any way related to love—how could it possibly be?

Hour after hour she tossed and turned, searching restlessly for the sleep that eluded her, as did the answer to how she could make her escape without jeopardising Libby, until exhaustion finally took over.

She had no idea how long she had slept when the subconscious churnings of her mind dragged her once more back to wakefulness. The discovery that it was scant minutes after three sent her stumbling, heavy-limbed with exhaustion, down to the kitchen.

She was halfway up the stairs, her tread slow and painstaking as she steadied her over-full mug of hot milk and honey she hoped would lull her back to sleep, when the sound of an opening door brought her to a halt.

There was scarcely any light, just what little filtered in from the security lights around the house, but the figure that had slipped from Michael's room, and now glided along the landing away from it, was small and slim and shapely. . .and most certainly not that of a man.

Ginny waited for what seemed like an eternity before continuing to her own room. She was glad, she told herself defiantly as she hauled her shock-numbed body back into bed; she was glad that she no longer needed to have any doubts about the sort of man she imagined herself to be in love with. Just because her heart felt as though it was breaking right now, didn't mean to say it was. . . Tomorrow her heart would be whole and able to hate him for the louse he was.

CHAPTER SIX

WHEN Aurelie left on her journey back to Paris late the following afternoon, the weather was still showing no sign of breaking.

Avoiding Michael and his vivacious accountant had not proved difficult as the two had spent their day, bar lunchtime, closeted in the makeshift office. But lunch had been purgatory, remembered Ginny bleakly, as she pressed her forehead against the window-pane and peered out into the stifling darkness.

Aurelie had been genuinely concerned by what had obviously been her zombie-like behaviour, thought Ginny with a shiver of disquiet, but had accepted the excuse of the oppressiveness of the heat with a spontaneous invitation for Ginny to accompany her back to Paris.

Ginny shook her head in mild disbelief at the memory. There was something decidedly bizarre about the whole thing: her being so tempted to leap at the chance of escape by courtesy of the woman whose relationship with Michael was, to a great extent, responsible for the horrific state to which she had been reduced, and Michael, laughing aside the suggestion while his eyes betrayed his anger at her obvious eagerness to go.

She rolled her forehead distractedly against the relative coolness of the glass and tried to recall what it was like to be sane, because her present state bore no relationship whatever to sanity, she thought despairingly: knowing what he was, knowing the despicable depths to which he could sink, yet being incapable of ridding herself of this terrible conviction that she loved him. She could almost hear her aunt's self-righteous words ringing in her ears, telling her this was the price she deserved to pay for her sins. . . Yet what sin had she ever committed to warrant a price as harsh as falling in love with just about the worst candidate she could possibly have picked?

She started back from the window with a cry of consternation as the lights of Michael's car swept blindingly across her line of vision. She couldn't face him. . .not yet. Perhaps not ever.

She ran to the kitchen, got out the casserole she had prepared earlier and put it in the oven. Panic flustering her, she picked up the pad by the telephone with the idea of leaving him a note to say she had gone to bed, then tossed it aside as the absurdity of such an action penetrated her panic. She raced into the hall and slap-bang into Michael.

'Now that's what I call a welcome,' he mocked, catching her against him and twirling her around.

'Put me down!' protested Ginny, pummelling angrily against him as a debilitating heat washed through her. 'I want to go to bed and——'

'And you're so happy to have me all to yourself again that you've come off your high horse and decided to invite me to join you.' There was laughter in his words, as he returned her to her feet, but the eyes holding hers were grim and humourless.

'I suppose that's your idea of a joke,' she hissed scathingly. 'What do you see women as—some sort of commodity, there simply to serve your needs?'

'If I do, what does that make you, Ginny?' he demanded harshly. 'And, though I'd never have put it as crudely as you've chosen to, the needs being served the other night were mutual.'

'And what about last night?' demanded Ginny, so consumed with anger that the words were out before she could stop them.

The look he gave her was both startled and wary. 'Well, one thing I can say about last night is that I sure as hell didn't get much sleep during it,' he drawled. 'And how about you, Ginny?'

'I slept like a log,' she lied frigidly.

'In other words, I might still want you but you've had all you want of me. Is that it, Ginny?' he enquired wryly. 'Don't worry, I don't intend putting that to the test. . . What I'd like right now, though, is to pick your brains.'

'Are you sure I have any brains worth picking?' lashed out Ginny, thoroughly disconcerted by his claim still to want her. 'Don't bother answering,' she added acidly. 'Whatever game this is—I'm not playing.'

'This isn't a game, it's business,' he snapped, taking hold of her arm as she made to move to the stairs.

'Isn't that why you employ qualified people like Aurelie?' she demanded scornfully, tearing free her arm. 'So that you can pick their brains?'

'Aurelie gives me what I ask of her, but I feel you might just be able to provide that little bit extra. You see——'

'No, I *don't* see!' howled Ginny, shrinking from him in horror. 'What sort of monster are you?'

'Now you're really confusing me,' he snapped. 'All I'm asking for is your advice.'

'My advice?' croaked Ginny, hooking her arm round the baluster to prevent herself collapsing in a heap.

'Perhaps more the unbiased view of a complete outsider, rather than actual advice, is what I'm looking for,' he conceded, his eyes narrowed and cool as they studied her. 'Look, how about if I explain over a pot of coffee? Or are you still hell-bent on getting to your bed?' He glanced down at his watch and pulled a face. 'You do realise, don't you, Ginny, that it's barely gone seven?'

'I haven't been sleeping well in this heat,' she muttered, her head swimming with confusion.

'Except for last night,' he murmured, 'when you slept like a log.'

'I. . . Yes, but it wasn't a refreshing sleep,' waffled Ginny, shrivelling with humiliation.

'Ginny, I really would be grateful if you'd hear me out and give me your view,' he coaxed, tilting his head to one side and producing a smile that not only wreaked havoc with her pulse-rate but resurrected every suspicion she had ever had concerning his proclivity for manipulation. 'I'll even make the coffee.'

'What—all by yourself?' drawled Ginny, her senses still reeling and her scalp still crawling from the mortification she had only herself to blame for as she turned and forced her legs back in the direction of the kitchen. All right, so she still hadn't learned how to control her feelings towards him. . . But, whatever they were, this was the man who had made passionate love to her one night and invited another woman into his bed the next.

'Honey, you're beginning to sound like me,' he chided from right behind her, 'and it doesn't suit you.'

'Then, obviously, the sooner I'm out of your company the better,' snapped Ginny. 'The last person I'd want to sound like is you—especially as you so often remind me of my aunt.'

'Oh, yes—that delightful aunt of yours you so hate,'

he muttered, filling a pan with water and putting it on to boil.

'I don't hate her,' protested Ginny.

'Well, you sure as hell don't like her,' he observed. 'Just as you don't like me. . . Or perhaps I'm kidding myself—perhaps I'm the one you hate,' he added with a grim laugh, reaching for the coffee-grinder.

'You don't need to grind any,' muttered Ginny, consoling herself that, the instant she regained her senses, hate would be too mild a word for her feelings towards him. 'There's some I did earlier—in that blue jar.'

'I don't notice you rushing to reassure me you don't hate me,' he drawled. 'Ginny, I warned you we could both end up regretting the other night,' he added more appeasingly.

'And you were right,' she retorted, what little rein she had left on her control slipping. 'It must be a wonderful sensation—knowing how right you always are!'

'I'm too modest a guy to take praise for stating the obvious,' he stated coldly, then shook his head in exasperation. 'Ginny, can't we cut out all this sniping?' he sighed. 'Let's just accept that we both know you're keeping something from me regarding Libby. OK, perhaps I over-reacted when she called yesterday morning and spun me that crazy yarn about a course she'd enrolled on and had tried to get out of to come down here and. . . Hell, a story's a story and I know when I'm being fed one. Ginny, what I'm trying to say is perhaps it's time you and I stopped letting Libby run our lives.'

'Libby never has run my life,' snapped Ginny, beginning to feel faint as her mind started alternating torrid memories of their lovemaking with those of Aurelie leaving his room.

'Ginny, don't pretend you don't know what I mean,' he said, walking up behind her and placing his hands on her shoulders. 'What happened between us the other night. . . Hey, Ginny, don't!' he exclaimed in horror as a sob choked from her.

'Stop it! Just leave me alone!' she choked, tearing herself free as he made to put his arms around her.

'Ginny, I never wanted things to turn out like this,' he protested.

'Didn't you?' she raged. 'Well, this is the way they are! I don't want you to touch me. . . I don't even want to be in the same room as you. . . I want to go home!'

'Home—to your loving aunt?' he demanded, a chilling sneer in his words. 'Nice try, Ginny, but I'm not quite the sucker for tears you plainly hoped I'd be.'

Ginny raised her tear-stained face to his in a look of utter horror. 'If you think I'd deliberately lower myself to this humiliating state in the hope you'd see reason, it only shows what sort of mind you have,' she choked. 'I'm sick and tired of trying to convince you that you've nothing to worry about over Libby and now I've had enough. . . Please let me leave!'

'The deal was that you stay till Libby shows up,' he stated implacably. 'If you want to leave, all you have to do is call her and tell her to come back.'

There was a grim set to his mouth as he brought cups and the coffee to the table, then sat down.

Feeling close to the end of her tether, Ginny also sat down. Her inexplicable bout of tears seemed mercifully over, but their mere fact disturbed her deeply. Tears were something her pride had strictly vetoed, where her aunt had been concerned; her crying had always been done in private and then exceptionally rarely.

'Here—have this,' Michael muttered, passing a cup of coffee to her.

Ginny rose and went to the fridge for milk.

'Sorry, I keep forgetting you take milk,' he muttered when she returned, his tone strained. 'I. . . Look, Ginny, I shouldn't have said what I did about you crying. Even in ideal circumstances, this sort of weather can fray the steadiest of nerves. Much more of this, and the odds are I'll be the one weeping on your shoulder—especially if I have any more business problems to contend with.'

'Your business—is it not doing well?' exclaimed Ginny, unable to mask her surprise.

'If by doing well you mean is it making money, it's doing abundantly well,' he murmured wryly. 'But money creates its own problems.'

'And this is what you wanted my opinion on?' asked Ginny sceptically.

He grinned as he nodded, then laughed when Ginny pulled a disbelieving face.

'It's one particular part of it I'd like your opinion on,' he said, 'but I'll need to fill you in on a bit of background information first.' He looked at her enquiringly and, when she said nothing, continued. 'Until just over two years ago our European banking subsidiaries were run by a Frenchman by the name of Henri Lachaise—you probably won't have heard of him, but he was a name to be reckoned with in international banking circles. Once I'd had the necessary experience in the States, I was to come here and be groomed by Henri to take over from him when he retired. I was still tied up in the States, but had started coming over here for a few months at a stretch—then

Henri died suddenly. My dad was very cut up about his death—those two went back a long way.'

'But you didn't come here right away,' said Ginny, remembering he had only been in Paris for a year.

'No. I was in the throes of tying up what I was doing in the States, preparatory to coming over here and working under Henri's guidance. My father came over for a short while, but he had too many commitments in the States to stay. He decided to let things tick over here under the existing management until I took over. You have to remember that I was stepping into the shoes of a pretty remarkable man and into a banking environment with which I still wasn't wholly familiar. So I set about familiarising myself. . . Damn it, I wound up knowing so much about the Paris outfit I probably could have told them when the air-conditioning was due for a service. I also found out that on three occasions, the first within months of Henri's death and the last a couple of months prior to my arrival, large sums had journeyed through a tortuous maze of accounts and eventually disappeared from sight. . . Delicately and discreetly, we had been robbed.'

'How can robbery be described as either delicate or discreet?' exclaimed Ginny, aghast.

'Oh, I promise you, it can,' he replied grimly. 'This particular scam is a veritable work of art—creative accounting at its very pinnacle.'

'And you want my opinion on this?' asked Ginny incredulously.

He laughed and shook his head. 'No—that was just the background.'

'Have you caught the people concerned?'

'There are two of them and they're known; but the police believe they're linked with perpetrators of similar thefts from other institutions and are therefore biding their time. Such a network makes tracing stolen money pretty difficult.'

'Is this still background?' asked Ginny.

'In other words, get to the point,' he murmured. 'OK. A while back, Aurelie, who is one of the few people in my confidence regarding this, picked up another sum that had sauntered off into the wide blue yonder——'

'Sorry,' cut in Ginny, 'but I don't understand what you mean by "sauntered off". Surely if money goes missing from an account, it's noticed immediately?' She had been tempted to ask why Aurelie happened to be one of the few in his confidence, simply to see what sort of answer he came up with, but found she hadn't the stomach to do so.

'International finance bears no resemblance to High Street banking—vast sums are being moved around all the time. Though at any stage during the shunting around of those three amounts that disappeared, I'm prepared to bet watertight cover would have been produced had any queries arisen—these guys plan faultlessly.'

'But they must have known they'd be caught in the end.'

Michael shrugged. 'They buried the thefts so deep there was a fair chance they wouldn't be unearthed, but they had the added incentive of knowing that if they were, the odds against pinning it on them were remote enough to warrant the risk. Deducing who had committed a crime is one thing, but proving it is another altogether. Anyway, what Aurelie unearthed proved quite a headache for the police. Compared with what had been taken before, this was an insignificant sum and the theft itself had none of the finesse of the others—the next audit would have brought it up at once. But the sum reappeared in the accounts before the next audit was due—and with the current rate of interest for the period it had been missing added to it.' His lips twitched in wry amusement at the look of incredulity on Ginny's face. 'Adding on that interest was like putting an asterisk against the transaction, demanding it be checked.'

'How long was the money missing?' asked Ginny, intrigued, yet thoroughly confused.

'A couple of weeks.'

'And it had nothing to do with the other thefts?'

'Nothing,' he confirmed, then reached over for the coffee-pot and refilled both their cups. 'But, to get to the point of all this—well, part of the point is that I resent the fact I'm keeping two crooks on my payroll so as not to jeopardise police investigations, yet I'm going to have to fire some kookie individual who steals my money, then pays it back with interest.'

'But they're two separate issues, aren't they?' puzzled Ginny, finding the point he was trying to make extremely elusive. 'And you'd have fired this other person anyway. . .wouldn't you?'

'I'd say that appropriating money from your employer, however briefly, was pretty good grounds for getting fired,' he retorted drily.

Ginny frowned suddenly. 'I gather this person hasn't yet been confronted.'

'Right.'

'So nobody actually knows why he did such a—well, to say the least, such a strange thing?'

'Does it matter why?' he asked, his eyes narrowed and watchful over the rim of his cup as he drank from it.

'Perhaps not to you—but it would to me,' replied

Ginny, her sympathies beginning to veer towards this anonymous person. 'He could have taken the money and run. Instead, he not only pays it back, he adds the interest to it, which, as you've admitted, makes what he's done stand out like a sore thumb. I could be completely wrong, and it probably sounds slightly crazy, but to me that indicates some sort of inherent honesty.'

'This he, by the way, is a she,' he muttered, staring moodily into the contents of his cup. 'So. . .what are you suggesting I do?'

Ginny glanced across at him, expecting to find sarcasm in his expression and feeling confused when she found none.

'I'm sorry, but I'm having difficulty believing you're actually asking me this,' she said.

He pulled a somewhat rueful face, then raked his fingers wearily through his hair. 'You probably can't imagine how difficult it is to keep a rational mind when circumstances force you to work with a couple of guys who have robbed you. I haven't just had to work with them during these past months; I've had to behave towards them as though they were a couple of regular guys and even socialise with them at times. I've had to keep down to the barest minimum the number of people who know, partly because I haven't been there long enough to be certain who I can trust, but also because some of those I know I could trust, I wouldn't want to risk putting under this sort of strain. I guess this latest thing was just the final straw, even though it's in no way related.'

'And is that why you came down here?' asked Ginny, having considerable difficulty stopping her sympathies overriding much greater considerations. 'To escape it all?'

'If you're asking me if I upped and fled down here—the answer's no,' he replied with a measure of amusement. 'I've let it be known for the past couple of months that I've been planning to come down here for a while. I've been careful not to make any sudden or unusual moves—even though the police are pretty sure my guys, and the others they're keeping tabs on, are convinced they've got away with it and are just sitting tight.'

'How on earth did you manage even to be civil to them?' asked Ginny, certain her reactions would have given the game away instantly.

'I didn't have any choice,' he retorted. 'There was too much riding on my behaving normally.' He glanced over at her, his look verging on hostile. 'But this place hasn't turned out the haven I'd anticipated.'

'You hoped you'd have Libby to talk things over with when you got here,' sighed Ginny, realising she would have felt pretty hostile towards him had their roles been reversed. 'Michael, I——'

'You still haven't said what you think I should do about my short-term borrower,' he cut in brusquely.

'I'd want to know why she borrowed the money before I made any decision,' she stated quietly.

He gave her a peculiarly blank look, then closed his eyes, tilted back his chair and sat in complete silence.

'You were the one who asked for my opinion,' said Ginny defensively after a while.

'And I can assure you, I don't have any problem with your opinion,' he muttered, righting his chair and taking a drink from his cup. 'I've had too many other things interfering with my judgement on this, and not least the police advising that I should make a big show of getting rid of her as fast as I can.'

'Well, if the police are already on the case——'

'Their interest is solely in the major case,' he cut in. 'They won't do anything on this one unless I press charges.'

'But you said they advised you to sack her.'

'They seem to think it might boost my two thieves' confidence if I got good and mad and make a big thing of firing her.'

'What? Make them think you'd have done the same if you'd found out about them and therefore make them sure you haven't?'

He pulled a wry face and nodded. 'Pretty dud psychology, if you ask me. I reckon the last thing those two crooks need is a confidence boost—they're too convinced of their own genius.' He gave a slightly weary shrug. 'The one thing I lost track of for a while—and which you pointed out to me—was that these are two very different cases—and that's how I have to treat them.'

'And I'm sure that's the advice Aurelie must have given you,' said Ginny, driven to mentioning the French girl as a means of reminding herself of exactly what he was, as the memories over which she had no control began stirring hot, reckless within her.

'Aurelie?' he queried abruptly. 'I neither ask for nor would I take kindly to the advice of my accountants on personnel matters.'

'I merely assumed that was the reason she came down here,' muttered Ginny stiffly. Silly her!

'I asked her down here regarding the other matter,' he stated, his look steely; then he removed from his shirt pocket the card Bernard de Maupéou had handed Ginny and gazed frowningly down at it before returning it to his pocket. 'I hope I don't need to stress that what I've told you this evening isn't to be discussed with anyone.'

'I'm hardly likely to broadcast it in the town square,' exclaimed Ginny, his words triggering an inexplicable anger in her. She rose to her feet. 'But you know what they say about a woman scorned,' she added recklessly, and could instantly have bitten off her tongue.

'Don't you think you've got that wrong?' he demanded, on her heels before she had reached the sink. 'I'm the one being scorned. . . I tell you how much I want you,' he murmured, his hands alighting on her shoulders, kneading them with a mesmerisingly sensuous touch, 'and you tell me not to touch you——'

'And I meant it,' ground out Ginny from between clenched teeth, her body leaping to his touch while every nerve in it became raw with the strain of creating the illusion of imperviousness.

'And I mean it when I tell myself not to touch you,' he breathed against her neck as his head lowered. 'But it doesn't mean I don't want to,' he whispered, his lips grazing tantalisingly against her skin. 'And when I do touch you, and your body trembles as it's trembling right now, I don't want my head to be filled with memories of you naked and passionate in my arms—but it is.'

It was the image his words triggered in her, of him lost in the throes of passion, but not with her, that brought an animal howl of outrage from her and gave her the strength to tear herself free.

'I also said I didn't want to be in the same room as you,' she told him, in a voice hoarse with emotion. 'And I meant that too!' She turned and walked to the door. 'There's a casserole in the oven and perhaps, while you're eating it, you can fill your damned head with memories of one of your other women—it's not as though you don't have plenty to choose from!'

CHAPTER SEVEN

MICHAEL was seated at the kitchen table when Ginny surfaced, the inevitable pot of coffee beside him, a wodge of print-out paper in his hand.

He looked up at her, his heavy-lidded eyes scrutinising her with a lazy malevolence that filled her with apprehension. She would have been better off not bothering to get out of the bed in which she had sweltered without sleep for most of the night, she told herself wearily, because whatever it was with which he was so obviously about to confront her, she was in no state to cope with it.

'I have to admit I'm very disappointed in you, Ginny,' he drawled. 'You're not quite the unsullied innocent you claim to be, are you?'

Not bothering to acknowledge his presence, and even less his goading words, Ginny took a glass from the dresser and went over to the fridge to pour herself some fruit juice.

'And as for the tales you told me about what brought you here,' he continued silkily, 'you forgot to mention this married guy you were involved with. Dear, oh, dear, what a scandal! The good news is that his wife's kicked him out. But ain't life a bitch, honey—here you are stuck with me and unable to go running back to him.'

'What are you drivelling on about?' asked Ginny, her exhausted mind dredging up half-hearted reminders of the investigation he had claimed to be making on her before retreating back into its state of virtual coma.

'Perhaps that's just as well, though,' he murmured, plainly enjoying himself too much to be deterred by her uncivil rejoinder. 'Most guys get mightily upset when they find their territory's been invaded and, you have to agree, I sure as hell have invaded his.'

'No doubt he'll be challenging you to pistols at dawn,' muttered Ginny, simply too exhausted to give vent to the anger seething within her.

'I wouldn't bank on that, if I were you, sweetheart,' he jeered, tossing aside the papers and picking up his coffee-cup. 'But never mind, Uncle Michael's taking you out on the town tonight,' he added with malevolent brightness, breaking off to take a mouthful from his cup. 'Which reminds me, we might take in a nightclub after eating——'

'As I shan't be coming with you, where you go after you've eaten doesn't concern me,' interrupted Ginny, then took a long drink of fruit juice in the hope it might restore at least some measure of energy to her.

'Ginny, we can do this the hard way, wasting time and energy hollering at one another for the next while, or you can do the sensible thing and accept right now that you and I are going out tonight,' he stated implacably. 'If it makes you feel any better, another couple will be joining us.'

Ginny leaned against the fridge clutching her empty glass and looking through leaden, hostile eyes at the man now leisurely helping himself to more coffee. The same sheen of perspiration she could feel on her own skin was visible on his, and there was that same, almost bruised darkness she had earlier detected around her own eyes surrounding his dark-lashed, heavy-lidded ones. On her it look haggard and unappealing, she thought with a sharp stab of resentment; on him it merely looked rakishly *louche* and only added to that element of danger in his dark good looks.

'Won't you mind it being obvious to your friends that I'm only there under duress?' she asked, her pride, while reluctantly accepting defeat, refusing to do so with any grace.

'Grow up, Ginny,' he drawled dismissively. 'But I doubt whether Bernard de Maupéou and his lawyer would notice, anyway.'

Ginny had to steel herself not to betray her reaction. The chances of his not knowing of the relationship between the banker and Jean-Claude verged on the non-existent, she reasoned with herself, but she certainly wasn't going to give him the satisfaction of betraying her shock at the idea of meeting him again. . . And as for his mentioning the man's bringing along his lawyer, she hadn't the slightest idea what that implied, nor of the effect, if any, he intended it to have on her.

'And what am I supposed to do, twiddle my thumbs while you three men discuss business?' she asked frostily.

'I'm glad to hear you've accepted you're coming,' murmured Michael smugly, 'and Bernard's lawyer, you should be pleased to hear, is a woman.'

'I should be pleased, should I?' demanded Ginny, wondering why on earth she was expending her energy on useless words, yet driven to keep doing so. 'I've been dragooned into an evening I've no wish whatever to participate in, so if you imagine I'm going to be pleased about any aspect of it, you're deluding yourself.'

She turned and opened the fridge, reached for a

yoghurt, then changed her mind. Things were bad enough without the stifling oppressiveness of the weather, she thought morosely—she hadn't even the energy to eat.

'Where are you going?' he demanded, as she began walking leaden-footed towards the door.

'I've got things to do in the garden,' she replied, trotting out the words with no regard to their content.

'Are you crazy?' he exclaimed, striding over to her. He took her by the arm and led her to a chair. 'You look bad enough as it is, without trying to kill yourself gardening in this weather,' he said, his hands pressing on her shoulders and forcing her down on to the chair. 'Besides, you haven't had any breakfast.'

'I don't want any,' she muttered as he walked away from her. She was almost comatose from lack of sleep: her head was swimming and, what was worse, she was teetering on the brink of tears once more. 'Michael, I've got to get away from here,' she pleaded hoarsely, 'this weather is killing me.'

'Your problem is lack of food,' he informed her tersely, placing fresh bread, butter and conserve before her. 'The last time you ate was lunch yesterday. And once you've got some of that down you, I suggest you get yourself some sleep—you look as though you've had none for a week.'

'Of course, it wouldn't do for someone as dashing as you to be seen in the company of a bleary-eyed wreck,' she muttered waspishly, spreading butter and black cherry jam liberally on a chunk of bread as hunger suddenly hit her. 'Perhaps it would be better if you left me behind.'

She nearly choked on the bread as his soft chuckle washed over and into her, seeping through her and filling her with sensuous chaos.

'I'm not leaving you behind,' he murmured, 'and you'd better get some sleep before this evening—unless you don't mind the fact that people will take one look at you and assume it's a surfeit of lovemaking making you look as you do.'

Her mind refused to come up with a suitably cutting retort; it was too busy trying to hold back the barrage of erotic memories those words had unleashed in her.

'If this weather doesn't break by tonight I'll be a stretcher case,' she managed eventually. 'Surely it can't go on like this much longer?'

'It shouldn't be too long now,' he said, returning to the chair opposite hers. 'There's a lot more thunder around. I hope you're not afraid of storms, because there's going to be an almighty one when this finally breaks.'

Ginny helped herself to more bread, noting with an uncharacteristic cynicism that now they were discussing the weather they were managing to be almost civil to one another. Great, she thought gloomily, now all she had to do was keep her mind and their conversation trained on the weather for the next few weeks and life would be a bed of roses.

'About tonight,' he said, 'I was thinking——' He broke off and rose as the telephone rang. He strode over to it. 'Well, well, if it isn't my elusive niece,' he drawled into the receiver, his eyes drilling across the room into Ginny's and sending her heart plummeting in the direction of the floor. 'Yes, she's right here—I've been standing over her making sure she eats her breakfast. . . No. . . OK, yes, I am bullying her, so why don't you do us all a favour and get your ass down here and stop me?'

Ginny rose to her feet, the anxiety pounding through

her for her friend blanking her mind of her own problems.

'You'd better talk to her,' Michael was saying. 'She's about to wrench the phone from my hand, anyway.' His expression one of glowering exasperation, he handed the receiver to Ginny. 'When you've finished, I'll be in the office,' he muttered, then turned and left the room.

'Ginny, what's gotten into him?' demanded Libby, her voice tight and edgy. 'He was fine the other times I spoke to him. . . Ginny, are you OK? What——'

'Libby, just calm down, will you?' said Ginny, her eyes widening in disbelief at the calm, unhurried sound of her own voice. 'The only problem down here is the weather—we've been teetering on the edge of a storm for the past few days and it's like living in a pressure-cooker.'

'But something must have happened,' protested Libby. 'He seemed OK with the excuse I gave him the other day—and now he's ordering me down there!'

'Libby, I hate to disillusion you, but he didn't believe a word of that story you fed him,' sighed Ginny.

'Oh, God, what am I going to do?' wailed Libby. 'You can't stay there—it's not fair on you. I should never have involved you in all this! Ginny, come to Paris——'

'Libby, you're getting yourself all worked up over nothing,' exclaimed Ginny, horrified by the obvious state her friend was in. 'Just calm down and listen to me.' Resolutely ignoring the protests already marshalling themselves in her mind, she took a deep breath and continued. 'He didn't believe your story but, apart from seeming a bit hurt about your not wanting to see him, he doesn't appear that put out.' She closed her eyes and took another deep breath. 'And though the weather really is a killer, he's probably in such a foul mood today because his girlfriend has just left.'

'She was there? You've met her?' exclaimed Libby, curiosity miraculously raising her spirits. 'What was she like? Is he really——?'

'Let me get a word in,' protested Ginny, her resolution beginning to waver as the image of Aurelie slipped into her mind: not the laughing, vivacious person she had so liked, but the shadowy figure that had emerged from Michael's room in the night. 'You'll love her,' she heard herself saying. 'She's bubbly and friendly. . . Her English is almost as bad as my French and we had hilarious times communicating. Honestly, Libby, I really liked her.' And she had, she thought bitterly—and still did, because none of this was in any way Aurelie's fault.

'And you really think he's in love with her?' asked Libby excitedly.

'For heaven's sake, Libby, how am I supposed to know?' she snapped, then immediately tried to make amends. 'Anyone who can even bear to hold hands in these steam-bath conditions must be in love, as far as I'm concerned—and they were all over one another,' she elaborated, grim-faced. 'Libby, you can't imagine how ghastly this weather is.'

'So come up here,' retorted Libby. 'Jeanne——'

'Libby, that contract you so blithely had me sign—it requires me to give a month's notice. Which is just as well,' she continued hastily, praying it wouldn't occur to Libby to wonder how she knew, 'because it means that during a spell like this, when I'd rather be anywhere but here, I'm not tempted to up and join you.'

'Ginny, we don't need the money he's paying you

that badly,' stated Libby firmly. 'If it came to it, I could always find a way of——'

'And if it comes to it, I'll be the first to let you know,' cut in Ginny, forcing amused exasperation into her tone. 'Are you sure your ego isn't just the teensiest bruised because Uncle Michael isn't kicking up the stink you anticipated?' Perhaps she should try for the stage, she thought, as her friend's shriek of protest greeted her words, stunned by her hitherto unsuspected talent for acting.

'Am I really sounding paranoid?' groaned Libby, when her shrieks of protest had subsided. 'Ginny, everything was going so great until Michael showed up. . . I just haven't been able to think straight since.'

A problem we both have had, thought Ginny miserably, while a fiercely protective love filled her as she remembered the almost evangelical determination with which Libby had changed her lifestyle for the sake of the baby she carried: the meticulous attention she paid to a healthy diet, her refusal to take so much as an aspirin when she had flu, the daily stint of softly soothing classical music—and now all this disruption and panic.

'Perhaps a few facts will help straighten out your thought processes,' she teased gently. 'First, Michael will be gone in next to no time. Second, he likes my cooking and hasn't complained about the garden, so our income is secure. Those were the pluses—on the minus side is the fact that I thought it wiser not to moonlight on my other gardening jobs while he's around, which means we really do need what I'm getting from him, no matter what you say. So, unless the man starts beating me black and blue and subjecting me to a third degree over you, what's the point rocking the boat?'

'Oh, Ginny. . . I don't know what to say,' choked Libby. 'I was so worried when Michael sounded so mad. But it isn't just that—Jeanne feels the same way you do about my not having let Jean-Claude know and, just like you, she hasn't pressed the point because she doesn't want to upset me. Ginny, I—'

'Hang on a moment, Libby,' cut in Ginny, her attention caught by the sound of a door closing, followed by footsteps. 'Michael's on his way back into the kitchen.'

'Good, I want to have another word with him.'

'You what?' exclaimed Ginny, as Michael entered the room.

'Don't worry,' laughed Libby, 'just let me speak with him. I miss you, Ginny—take care. Now give me Michael.'

'And you take care, too,' said Ginny, and turned to Michael. 'Libby would like another word with you.'

'Is that so?' he drawled unenthusiastically, taking the receiver from her. 'Libby, I've already. . . I what?' He glanced over at Ginny, who was clearing the table, an expression of reluctant amusement on his face. 'She's right, it's bad, but it should break soon.'

Ginny took the dishes to the sink, his silence making her wonder what on earth Libby could be saying that was taking so long.

'She's fine. Once she's finished cooking steak and fries for my lunch, I'm sending her to the garden to dig over part of it. . . No? Well, maybe you should get down here and check for yourself. . . OK, OK. . . No, I don't, but you take care of yourself anyway.'

Whatever she had been saying, Libby had managed to get round him to the extent that he was no longer growling at her, noted Ginny, as she rinsed the dishes—which was all very well for Libby, tucked safely away in Paris and not having to face him.

'About tonight,' he said from the doorway. 'Have you something suitable to wear?'

It took a couple of seconds for his words to sink in, then Ginny felt her cheeks flame with indignation. 'I thought I'd wear my dungarees,' she said through clenched teeth.

'Because if you haven't,' he continued, disdainfully ignoring her reply, 'we'll have to go into Cannes and get you something.'

'We're not going anywhere to get me anything. I'm perfectly happy with the clothes I have, and if you're not—tough,' she retorted, flinging the cutlery she had just rinsed down on the draining-board. 'If you're so worried about appearances, you should have thought about that before ordering someone like me to accompany you.'

'Well, if you do decide on the dungarees,' he murmured, 'try them without the T-shirt—that should turn a few heads and it might even start a trend.'

Ginny didn't give even a moment's thought to what she would wear when she got to her room. Her eyes were drooping with fatigue as she undressed and flopped down on to the bed. With the almost constant background of thunder rumbling softly around her, she slid unresistingly into a heavy dreamless sleep and remained there for several hours.

She awoke feeling heavy-limbed and muggy-headed, and staggered to the shower, where she stood under freezing water for as long as she could bear it.

Feeling almost refreshed, she consulted her watch and gave a gasp when she saw the hour. No time to dither over what she was going to wear, she thought frustratedly, flinging open her wardrobe and deciding, as she viewed its meagre contents, that she had better raid Libby's far more substantial range. She paused, her eyes widening as they alighted on an item tucked away at the back. She hesitated, battling with a peculiar reluctance, then removed it from the cupboard. She had honestly forgotten she had brought it with her, she thought, as she removed the dress from its transparent protection—this most suitable dress, this dream dress that had cost her what had seemed a fortune and which she had possessed for well over a year and still not worn.

She closed her eyes and buried her face in the floaty softness of the material, wondering if she had blotted it from her mind because of a subconscious loathing to squander her first wearing of her dream dress on an evening she was dreading.

Her dream dress, she thought bitterly—just how childish could she get? She sat down on the bed, clutching the dress to her, a bitter, aching loneliness filling her as she remembered when she had bought it, and all the other times as a child, when desperation had driven her to buying herself small presents, a book or a pot of flowers, and pretending to herself they were gifts from her beloved parents. But she hadn't resorted to that since she was about fifteen, until the day she had bought this dress—the day she had overheard her aunt talking about an unruly, promiscuous teenager to a new member of her bridge circle, without at first realising that the girl being discussed was herself.

Perhaps she should have bought a scarlet dress, thought Ginny bitterly as, with trembling hands she slipped it over her head. Though black was probably just as damning as scarlet as far as her aunt was concerned, she supposed, as she zipped up the dress.

She twirled around, luxuriating in the gossamer

fineness of the material as she walked to the full-length mirror. Her expression crumbled to one of bemused uncertainty as she regarded her reflection.

For reasons she was unable to fathom, she had tried on the dress once and only once—in the shop on the day she had bought it. On that single occasion she had felt like a fairy princess and now, despite the oddly ambivalent, almost superstitious reservations she had always had about actually wearing it, something seemed to be telling her that tonight was the night she needed this dress and all it did for her. All right, she admitted wryly, as she began lightly making up her face, it was her pride that needed it; and pride that had taken the sort of battering hers had needed all the indulging it could get.

But there was an almost haunted expression on her face as she inspected her reflection, her hands darting nervously from the close-fitting bodice of the dress to the deep V of its neckline. Beautiful though this dress was, it really wasn't her, she thought agitatedly, as she attempted to draw most of the material across the sun-kissed swell of her breasts—it was far too low-cut, for a start!

'Ginny!'

She started with fright at the bellowed summons emanating from the hall below.

'I'm coming!' she called out, flying to the wardrobe in sudden panic.

It was a straw-coloured cashmere stole Libby had sent her a couple of Christmases ago that caught her eye.

'Ginny—I'm going out to the car!'

Accepting that she simply hadn't the time to change into anything else, she flung the stole over what she was beginning to regard as her near-nakedness. Then she slipped on a pair of black, high-heeled sandals and sped from the room.

'I thought you said you were going to the car,' she blurted out in defensive accusation, as she began descending the stairs and saw Michael waiting at the foot.

'I was just trying to hurry you.'

Her steps faltered as the words reached her, any last vestige of confidence deserting her beneath the dark-eyed scrutiny of the dinner-jacketed man awaiting her.

All the flattering dresses in the world couldn't alter anything, she told herself defeatedly; couldn't alter the fact that she was hopelessly in love with a complete jerk, nor the fact that she was going to be completely out of her depth in the company of such worldly sophisticates as this man and his artistocratic French counterpart.

He was looking up at her as she descended the last few stairs and there was something in his eyes that brought a suffocating tightness to her chest.

He reached out a hand to her, which she ignored because her own were occupied keeping the stole firmly around her.

'Tell me, Ginny,' he drawled, 'is that wrap hiding a surprise—such as an old T-shirt?'

He turned and walked towards the door.

So much for her vivid imagination, thought Ginny bitterly as she followed, and as for her starry-eyed vision of herself as a fairy-tale princess—she couldn't have made less of an impression on him had she actually worn her dungarees.

'Do you plan on maintaining this lamb being led to the slaughter look all evening?' enquired Michael, as he launched the powerful car down the drive with a speed Ginny found alarming.

'Probably,' retorted Ginny, snatching a glance at his grimly aloof profile. She turned away as she began seeing that same face, hovering above hers as it once had, its chiselled perfection distorted by passion. 'Why should I pretend?'

'Why should you, indeed?' he murmured, then lapsed into silence.

Ginny stared out into the darkness, wondering desolately what lay ahead of her—not just tonight, but in the years to come. Something had been torn apart in her and what she feared most was that she was kidding herself that she could begin to regain her freedom once Michael was gone. What she now craved was a categorical assurance that the day would come when she would be free; when she was no longer being constantly caught off guard by vividly intimate memories of being made love to by a man she wanted to hate but had somehow come to love.

'So, what's he like?' he asked out of the blue, a long while later. 'Bernard de Maupéou?'

Ginny tensed. She had avoided thinking about the Frenchman; now she wondered if she hadn't simply created more problems for herself by not mentioning it had been Libby he had originally come to see. She gave a mental shrug—why bother, when whatever she did was bound to be wrong?

'He's fiftyish,' she said, 'not particularly tall, and——'

'I wasn't asking you what he looked like,' snapped Michael. 'I'll be able to judge that for myself in a while.'

'I only met the man for a few minutes,' replied Ginny, peering out of the window and realising, as the car entered the Boulevard de la Croisette, that they were already in Cannes. 'But I'm sure you'll get on very well with him.'

'I guess that's your not too subtle way of telling me you didn't like the guy,' laughed Michael, slowing the car right down, then swinging it into the porticoed entrance of a luxury hotel. He brought the car to a halt, exchanged a few words with the uniformed doorman who approached, then turned to her, grinning. 'What did he do, make a pass at you, Ginny?'

'When I said I thought you'd get on with Monsieur de Maupéou,' Ginny informed him frigidly, 'I didn't mean to imply that he was in any way like you.'

'I'm sure you didn't,' he murmured piously. 'But you shouldn't blame me for asking.'

Not having the slightest idea what he meant, Ginny made do with giving him a scathing look.

'Ginny, that's what I meant this morning about us guys not liking our territory invaded,' he explained, his expression a parody of wide-eyed innocence. 'So I guess this means I'm getting territorial over you. . . Now, wouldn't that make a great song title?' he sighed, and batted his eyelashes at her with mocking extravagance. Then he turned and motioned the doorman over. 'Come on, out you get—this guy needs to park the car.'

Grim-faced, Ginny got out of the car, instantly hankering after its air-conditioning as she stepped into what felt like a steam-bath. Sweltering beneath the stole still clutched firmly around her, she joined Michael, who was eyeing her incredulously from halfway up the steps.

'For God's sake, Ginny, do you have to wear that blanket?' he demanded, taking her arm.

'Yes!' snapped Ginny, tearing herself free.

'OK, you've made your point,' he informed her

icily, his fingers biting into her flesh beneath the softness of the cashmere as he took her once again by the arm and hauled her up the rest of the steps, 'but that's enough—understood?'

'And what will you do if it isn't?' demanded Ginny recklessly, then pulled up sharply with a gasp of consternation as, startlingly out of the blue, it occurred to her that she hadn't told Libby about Bernard de Maupéou's visit.

'Ginny, what's wrong?' he exclaimed, turning to her in alarm.

'I. . . Nothing,' she muttered, even more thrown by his spontaneous concern than she had been by her sudden memory of her omission.

'You're sure?' he persisted, his eyes confusing her with the warmth of their concern.

'I'm sure,' she replied, her eyes dropping from his for fear of what her own might betray. 'And don't worry, I'll try to remember all the social graces my aunt instilled in me—tonight I'll endeavour to behave in a manner with which neither of you could find fault.'

'Do me a favour, will you, Ginny?' he rasped, as the palatial doors of the hotel opened to receive them. 'Don't ever mention my name in the same breath as that woman's again.'

CHAPTER EIGHT

'WHY don't you come and sit next to me so that you can see the dancing?' suggested Bernard de Maupéou, amusement twinkling in the shrewd grey-blue of this eyes. 'Francine and Michael make a spectacular couple.'

'I'm feeling far too lazy to move even that far,' replied Ginny, smiling across the table at the banker and marvelling that she no longer felt in the least intimidated by the air of world-weary sophistication he exuded.

The evening had started disastrously; she had walked into it with her mind traipsing from one to another of a mass of disparate worries, attempting to spread her attention between them all like a meticulous hostess circulating among her guests. Her thoughts about Michael were such that she was constantly having to conjure up images of Aurelie leaving his room in her desperation to combat them. Then, there was her not having mentioned Bernard's visit to Libby, an oversight that she had mentally blown out of all proportion, illogically expecting the Frenchman to confront her with it each time he addressed her. It was only when she finally began relaxing that reason returned to her and she was able to put it from her mind.

'My dear, perhaps I was being tactless,' murmured Bernard, leaning concernedly across the table towards her, 'mentioning what an attractive couple Michael and Francine make.'

'What on earth makes you say that?' asked Ginny, acutely conscious of the colour that had immediately rushed to her cheeks.

'You're not jealous?' he enquired.

'I've no reason to be,' she lied. Aurelie, Francine—the list was probably so long she would die of exhaustion if she kept up this intensity of jealousy over them all, she reasoned bitterly, then added as a concerned afterthought, 'Heavens, I didn't think! Are you?'

'What—jealous over Francine?' he chortled, plainly most amused. 'My dear, I'm a disgustingly happily married man and not in the least given to chasing other women. Francine does work for me, but if she weren't my niece—the daughter of my wife's sister, that is—I wouldn't have considered bringing her here. A man of my years,' he murmured, rolling his eyes in mock horror, 'escorting an employee of Francine's youth—my, that really would set a few tongues wagging.'

'I'm sorry,' murmured Ginny with an apologetic grimace. 'Is your wife not down here with you?'

'I only wish she were,' he sighed. 'But my Renée is in Zurich, visiting her mother, who has just had a minor operation. I can't stand Paris when she's not around, which is why I headed south.' He glanced down at his watch, then looked back at her with a smile. 'Once Michael and Francine get back, I shall make my nightly call to her. She rings me in the morning and I ring her at night when we're apart.'

'Why wait for them?' exclaimed Ginny, touched by his open affection for his wife, so at odds with the air he generated, and finding it increasingly difficult to believe she had ever found him so intimidating. 'It's late—you go and ring her now.'

After a few half-hearted protests, he agreed, promising not to be gone for long. Ginny was still smiling as he disappeared from her view. She was glad to have been so wrong about him, she thought, remembering the feelings almost of panic that had filled her when, on entering the hotel, she had first caught sight of him and the stunningly attractive Francine. Yet it had been Bernard who had gone out of his way to make her feel at ease; apologising, where Michael hadn't bothered attempting to, for leaving her stranded for the half an hour he and the American had disappeared soon after they had all met. Admittedly they had left her with Francine, but the French girl had spotted an old friend in a group and had spent most of the time talking to him. No explanation had been offered for the two men's disappearance, but Ginny felt certain they had gone off alone to discuss Libby and Jean-Claude—a certainty that had filled her with unease and foreboding until she had managed to cast that too from her mind. And it had been Bernard who, perhaps noticing her reluctance when Francine had suggested they visit the hotel casino after they had eaten, had expressed a preference for the piano bar. Not being in a position to afford to gamble, even had she had any money on her, Ginny had gratefully endorsed his suggestion—though the discovery that the piano bar was an intimate, dimly lit and, given the time of year, surprisingly well-patronised nightclub, had made her feel vaguely uneasy.

'My wife says I must tell you I need exercise,' announced the beaming Frenchman when he returned, 'then you might take pity on me and dance with me.'

Ginny hesitated. 'It's not that I wouldn't like to try but, to be honest, the reason I refused earlier is that I'm not any good at it.'

Bernard de Maupéou looked slightly taken aback

for an instant, then threw back his head and laughed. He reached out a hand to her.

Though a little disconcerted, Ginny placed her hand in his. 'Let's hope you can laugh this heartily once your feet discover I wasn't being in the least modest.'

'I'm not much of a dancer,' he assured her, urging her to her feet. 'I merely shuffle around with an air of supreme, and grossly misplaced, confidence.' He paused, his expression suddenly quizzical. 'But I doubt if either of us will be able to shuffle with much success if you intend remaining swaddled as you have been all evening.'

Ginny felt herself blush to her roots. Sweltering though she now was beneath it, the stole had become like a second skin that she had all but forgotten.

'Oh, dear—there isn't a reason for your not wanting to remove it, is there?' he asked with mild concern.

Ginny shook her head, removing the stole and feeling faintly ridiculous for having clung to it for so long. And now that she thought about it, the neckline of her dress, the cause of her earlier misgiving, was almost prim compared with some she had seen that evening.

There was an expression of amused exasperation on Bernard's face as he gazed down at her, shaking his head.

'What a strange girl you are,' he sighed, tucking her arm through his.

'What do you mean?'

'It occurred to me for one terrible moment that there might be a disfiguring scar or a birthmark you wished to hide,' he replied, as he led her towards the dance-floor. 'My dear, if there's one thing I love, it's a good mystery to unravel,' he added with a chuckle.

'And you think you've found one, do you?' smiled Ginny, though her heart had sunk.

'I do believe I have,' he chuckled, as they joined what had become quite a crowd. 'Ginny, were you serious when you said you couldn't dance?'

'Extremely.'

'Right—the secret is to go limp and simply follow my lead.'

'I think that might be a problem—I don't find following in the least simple.'

'That, my dear, is why you must go completely limp—like a rag doll,' announced Bernard, sweeping her into his arms and promptly treading on one of her feet. 'You see,' he admonished, 'you weren't limp enough.'

After several false starts, Ginny was amazed to find herself relaxed enough to be able to follow the subtle guidance of a man she suspected was actually a very good dancer.

'We're doing so well,' he murmured teasingly after a while, 'I think we can now risk introducing conversation into the exercise. . . We'll start with the mystery.'

Ginny disrupted things for a few seconds by missing a beat. Not only did his talk of mysteries make her feel apprehensive, but her not having passed his message on to Libby had again raised its head from out of the blue. Had he even once, during the course of the evening, mentioned Libby's name, she might have felt able to broach the subject with him, she reasoned uncomfortably with herself; but he hadn't and she didn't feel able.

'Limp, my dear. Completely and utterly limp,' he chided teasingly. 'That's better. . . Now, to the mystery. What possible reason can there be for a beautiful creature to spend most of the evening huddled under a horse-blanket?'

'Horse-blanket?' protested Ginny, relief flooding through her. 'That happens to be a cashmere stole! And anyway, I'd forgotten I was wearing it.'

'Fibber,' he laughed. 'I think that this delightful creature was labouring under the ludicrous belief that she was successfully hiding her beauty from. . . Well, certainly not me, and even more certainly not Francine.'

'Very astute,' murmured Ginny, her relief instantly cancelled as she realised that this indeed very astute man might be only too capable of putting two and two together. 'I'm afraid I was being rather childish—you see, Michael's used to seeing me in my gardening clothes and——'

'Your what?' he exclaimed. 'I'm sorry, but did I hear you correctly?'

'You did. I must have forgotten to tell you I'm Michael's gardener,' murmured Ginny, beginning almost to enjoy herself.'

'And I'm his chauffeur,' retorted Bernard drily, but he missed a step and had to execute some neat footwork to avert a disaster.

'Honestly, Bernard, I'm not joking,' protested Ginny. 'I also cook for him.'

'But you told me you were a friend of his niece,' stated Bernard, the warmth beginning to drift from his tone.

'And I am. It was Libby who originally hired me on behalf of the estate—I needed a job.'

'All right, so Michael is used to seeing you in your gardening clothes,' he recapped warily.

Ginny closed her eyes momentarily; how was it that

she always managed to make a complete mess of even a simple thing like this?

'Well, to be honest, he annoyed me by asking if I had anything suitable to wear for tonight,' she said, the truth bursting out of her unintended and being rewarded by a warm chuckle. Encouraged, she continued. 'The reason I put on the stole initially was because. . . Well, I felt this dress was a little too low-cut. When Michael saw me all wrapped up, he was immediately suspicious—he thought I might be wearing something ghastly, like an old T-shirt under it, just to annoy him.'

'And so you kept yourself wrapped up until now,' chuckled Bernard, 'just to keep him guessing. Ginny, forgive me for saying it, but your relationship with Michael strikes me as exceedingly——'

'So this is where you two have got to.'

Ginny froze with shock as Michael's familiar voice spoke from directly behind her.

'Go away,' growled Bernard, marking time to the slow beat of the music.

'Now, now, Bernard, don't be so unsociable,' chided Michael, the soft laugh accompanying his words sending a caressing shiver ripply down Ginny's spine. 'Francine and I have decided it's about time we tried new partners.'

'Well, don't let us stop you,' murmured Bernard, his eyes twinkling as they met Ginny's. 'Your gardener and I wish to continue our fascinating conversation.'

'Keep to the rules, Bernard,' laughed Michael. 'You're supposed to——'

The rest of his words were lost to Ginny as she was expertly swept off into the throng of dancing couples. But the thing that troubled her most about that brief encounter was the ridiculous sensation now assailing her of having just been rescued from unspeakable danger.

'It was probably unforgivably rude of me to behave like that,' murmured Bernard, 'but I didn't wish to lose you before unravelling the rest of the mystery.'

'I thought we'd unravelled it all,' said Ginny, striving to recapture the feelings of ease which had so swiftly deserted her, but not helped by the barely perceptible change in her partner's tone.

'Perhaps there are some things better left unravelled,' he stated quietly, 'and besides, your relationship with Michael is none of my business. I am probably stretching a point to claim that your relationship with his niece is my business, but as she is to become part of my family, I feel it is.'

'I have a very good relationship with Libby,' protested Ginny, the now-familiar feeling of being unbearably trapped once more assailing her. 'She's my dearest friend.'

'Yet you have no way of contacting her; you can't even remember the name of the people she's staying with,' he pointed out ominously. 'And not once this evening have you so much as mentioned her name. I have a strong sense of intuition—and it's telling me something isn't quite right.'

Ginny felt his arm tighten supportively around her as the wave of bitterness washing over her brought a leaden clumsiness to her feet.

'Don't you mean it's Michael telling you something isn't quite right? That his niece refuses to see him and he doesn't know where she is!' she burst out, sick with disappointment. What a fool she was not to suspect something like this, she told herself angrily—it was obviously the whole point of this charade of an evening.

'Ginny, I haven't the slightest idea what you're talking about,' he exclaimed sharply, 'and I'd like an explanation immediately.'

'Do you honestly think I don't know why you and Michael went off in a huddle the moment we got here?' she demanded bitterly. 'You must have told him about the separation and the fact that they'll be getting married once——'

'Ginny, I am not at liberty to tell you what Michael and I were discussing, but Libby didn't enter into it at all,' he interrupted curtly. 'Now, for heaven's sake, tell me what this is all about.'

'You weren't discussing Libby?' she croaked weakly.

'We were discussing a rather unpleasant matter affecting both our businesses,' he sighed. 'I'm afraid that's all I can say—but I can assure you, we didn't discuss your friend.'

Ginny felt faint as she realised exactly what it was they must have been discussing—the thefts Michael had told her about; Bernard's must have been one of the other institutions affected. And now she had again put her foot in it and made things ten times worse than they need ever have been.

'I just don't know where to begin apologising,' she exclaimed dejectedly. 'Libby's relationship with the Grants has never been good, but she wants to change all that once she and Jean-Claude are together.'

'But from what you've said, I gather she hasn't even informed them she and Jean-Claude are to marry.'

'She hasn't,' sighed Ginny. 'I can't claim to know the way her mind works, but Jean-Claude has become the most important thing in her life and it's—it's almost as though she's marking time, not facing any of the things she should, until he's back.'

'And meanwhile, poor little Ginny is left to pacify a

totally bemused uncle,' he chuckled softly. 'I'm sure the last thing my sister and her husband intended was for the separation to create all this chaos. Poor little Ginny, no wonder you——'

'Time to change partners, folks—and this time no arguing!'

It happened so quickly that Ginny wondered if she hadn't momentarily blanked out. One moment she was in Bernard's arms, relieved to find him so understanding—the next she was in Michael's, being spun giddily away and feeling anything but relieved.

'Now that you've dispensed with the blanket,' he murmured, his eyes dark and sultry in their appreciation as he held her momentarily from him, 'I'm glad you didn't opt for the dungarees.'

'Michael, I'm useless at dancing. I——'

'Ginny, the success of a lie depends a lot on its being at least mildly credible,' he murmured, drawing her closely against him. 'I've been watching you and Bernard smooching around the floor too long for that one to stand a chance.'

Relax, she chanted to herself, as his presence began permeating her entire being with a drug-like, melting weakness; the secret is to go completely limp—like a rag doll.

'But you haven't been watching me, have you, Ginny?' he continued, his chin nuzzling lightly against her head. 'Seeing you so wrapped up in Bernard started up a few more of those territorial problems I keep getting over you. What were you guys talking about, anyway?'

'I wasn't wrapped up in Bernard,' retorted Ginny, furious to find her heart racing excitedly over his mocking reference to jealousy. 'Apart from the fact that he happens to be a happily. . .' Her entire body froze as she realised what her thoughtless words had left her open to, and brought them both to an awkward halt as her feet become entangled with his.

'A happily what, Ginny?' he enquired innocently. 'Were you about to say married man?'

'I want to go back to the table,' she protested weakly, 'I've told you I can't dance, and——'

'And I can only believe my eyes,' he murmured, pulling her body so close to his that they might have been one. 'You danced with Bernard. . .and now you'll dance with me.'

It was impossible not to follow him, she thought distractedly, as her body began responding to every nuance of his, not when they were practically glued together like this. And this most certainly wasn't the way Bernard had danced; this was an uninhibitedly sensuous interaction with the slow, throbbing beat of the music that was affecting her in a mind-blowingly erotic way.

'So you can't dance?' he murmured, his head lowering to bring his cheek against her temple.

'I couldn't until tonight,' croaked Ginny, vivid memories of their lovemaking torturing her as her every sense soaked in his presence.

'Until Bernard waved his magic wand.'

'I. . . What little experience I've had with dancing has usually been disastrous—I mean, until tonight.'

'So I was right. Bernard obviously has a magic touch,' he drawled.

'He merely pointed out the necessity of relaxing,' retorted Ginny, relieved to hear her words sounding a little more controlled, but still convinced she was about to explode with the tension gripping her.

'And you're feeling relaxed right now, are you, Ginny?' he taunted softly, his lips playing against her hair while his body held hers captive in the languid sensuality of its rhythmic movements.

'I'm only dancing with you because it would have been impolite to refuse,' she muttered defensively, while inwardly despairing of the perversion in her nature that could override all reason and keep her craving for him like a sex-driven robot. And when the ghost of Aurelie refused to come to her assistance, she felt as though she had been abandoned in a hell from which there was no escape.

'Tell me, Ginny,' he mocked softly, his arms tightening barely perceptibly around her, 'do you honestly think we present a picture of a couple having a duty dance?'

'What sort of picture did you and Francine present?' The bitterness and jealousy in those blurted-out words roared in her ears, but there was no taking them back.

'I can assure you I didn't dance quite like this with Francine, but you wouldn't know, would you, Ginny?'

'Well, this is exactly the way I danced with Bernard,' she retorted, ignoring his barbed question.

'I hope not,' he muttered. 'He being a happily married man. But why is it that, while I couldn't take my eyes off you dancing with him, you never once looked in my direction? Was it because you were so wrapped up in him, or was it your reluctance to see me with another woman in my arms that kept your eyes glued to him?'

She hadn't wanted to see him with the stunning Francine in his arms and, like a wishful child, had made certain she didn't, she admitted angrily to herself; but seen or unseen, Francine or Aurelie—fact was fact.

'If you need any help answering, it would make life

a darned sight easier on me if you opted for Bernard,' he persisted.

'What makes you think I'd want to make life easier for you?' she retorted, and felt a lump catch in her throat when the softness of his answering chuckle rippled through her in a discomfiting mixture of pleasure and pain. It was crazy—sick!

'I know you want to make it as hard as you possibly can for me,' he murmured against her hair. 'Of course, you don't need me to tell you how well you're succeeding.'

'And you don't need me to tell you that you're talking a load of rubbish,' replied Ginny wearily, and gave a sharp gasp as his arms tightened angrily around her.

'OK, I'm talking a load of rubbish,' he rasped against her ear. 'So tonight we go home and continue from here—is that how it's going to be?'

'Michael, stop this!' she begged, too many conflicting emotions assailing her for her even to attempt to make sense of his words. 'I don't know what you mean.'

'OK, I'll spell it out for you,' he said, his suffocating hold on her not letting up as he tilted back his head and gazed down at her from eyes that smouldered with both anger and passion. 'You and I have spent a night in one another's arms—or had you forgotten, Ginny?' he demanded huskily, his head lowering towards hers as though he were about to kiss her. As though only just realising what he was doing, he gave a small shake of his head and drew back from her. 'No, you haven't forgotten any more than I have. And you can tell me all the lies and half-truths you like, but your body will never be able to lie to mine. Just as it isn't lying now.'

'Please, Michael,' she pleaded barely audibly, 'don't do this to me.'

'I'm doing no more to you than you are to me—telling you how badly I need you.' Anger suddenly sharpened his tone. 'But unlike you, I shan't be playing the prissy innocent in a few hours' time, denying that right now all either of us wants is to be alone to make love as——'

'No!' she cried out sharply, causing several heads to turn in their direction.

'What are you denying, Ginny?' he snarled. 'I guess you're telling me you won't be giving me another brush-off, because you sure as hell can't deny you're ripe for lovemaking right this——'

'Ripe?' she hissed, having to make a conscious effort not to scream out the word at him. 'What am I—just another piece of fruit in a basketful of women? What does Francine need, another couple of days to ripen to your pleasure? And what about Aurelie——?'

Her demented outburst came to a stifled halt as he placed his hand on the nape of her neck and wedged her head firmly against him.

'If you want to rant and yell, that's OK by me,' he informed her severely, 'but as I'm not about to become part of a public scene, you'll have to save it till later—understood?'

Mortified beyond description, Ginny tried to nod, but couldn't because of his vice-like hold on her neck. She brought her arms from around him and wedged them against his chest, trying to push herself free enough to speak.

'Ginny, I'm warning you,' he growled angrily, releasing her head and taking her by the shoulders, 'if——'

'I couldn't breathe, let alone speak,' she gasped. 'Michael, please. . . I want to leave.'

'Bernard and Francine have just returned to the table,' he informed her icily, 'and we are going to join them. Until we find an appropriate time to say our farewells, you are going to stay put and behave like a reasonably responsible human being. . . Have I made myself clear?'

'Perfectly,' she replied, feeling limp and slightly dazed from the shock of her outburst.

She glanced up at him, as he took her firmly by the arm and eased her towards their table through the swathe of dancers, and saw the tight-lipped grimness of his expression. So this was the sort of man she imagined herself to be in love with, she thought with disgust, a man whose understanding of the concept of honour went no deeper than fretting that his might be tarnished by a public scene!

'Good timing,' Bernard greeted them. 'I've just ordered coffee. Francine and I will have to leave shortly—the waiter tells us the storm has at last broken and it's like the deluge out there.'

'About time too,' muttered Michael, seeing Ginny to her chair, then flopping down on his. 'I've never known weather get to me like this.'

'Well, for future reference, I feel I should report to you that I found your—er—gardener out working in it when I visited the other day,' murmured Bernard innocently. 'Poor little scrap—you really should look after her better, Michael. I can think of a dozen or so people who wouldn't be above head-hunting her from you.'

'They'd be wasting their time,' murmured Michael, his eyes on the waiter arriving with the coffee. 'Ginny just loves working for me, don't you, honey?'

'Honey?' queried Francine, rolling her eyes questioningly at Ginny. 'Sounds almost as sexist as dear old Uncle Bernard here,' she chuckled. 'Or do you call Michael honey too, Ginny?'

'Oh, I call him a lot of things,' murmured Ginny airily, so relieved to be out of the danger of his arms that she was feeling almost giddy. 'And talking of uncles,' she added, tossing all caution to the wind, 'I forgot to tell you, Michael, Bernard is Jean-Claude's uncle—though you probably already know that.'

'I probably do,' he muttered non-committally.

'And another thing,' she said, turning to the Frenchman. 'I've spoken to Libby since we last met but, what with one thing and another, it went clean out of my mind to tell her you had called. But I promise I'll tell her next time we speak.' She was gabbling, she thought uncomfortably; it was obvious from the slightly wary looks both Bernard and Francine were giving her, but she couldn't stop. 'I feel so terrible I forgot to tell her. I'm sure she'd have been thrilled to hear you'd dropped in, and most sorry to have missed you.'

'So it seems this romance is still very much on,' said Michael, when Ginny paused, preparatory to gabbling further.

Bernard gave a wry smile, though the look he gave Ginny was still somewhat wary. 'Very much so,' he murmured. 'They're not apart of their own choosing, but it will probably do them more good than harm.'

Ginny watched Michael's face, as Bernard explained the year's separation, and found it entirely expressionless.

'It must be very handy,' murmured Francine to Ginny in a bored aside, 'having an oil rig out on the high seas to which you can send a wayward son to shape him up.'

Ginny ignored the remark; she was listening to Bernard and was surprised to hear that he had finished—without having mentioned that his nephew and Libby intended marrying the moment their period of separation was finished. Then she decided it wasn't that surprising—Bernard would hardly consider it his place to tell Michael such news if his niece hadn't chosen to do so.

'Well, the moment Libby decides to show up, we can all have a get-together,' Michael was saying with no sign of rancour. 'If not down here, then at my place in Paris.' He turned to Ginny. 'Would you like more coffee?'

She shook her head. 'No, thank you.'

'Well, I think it's time we made a move—we've a storm to negotiate.'

Francine and Bernard rose too.

'I think you'll find that you might be needing this after all,' chuckled Bernard, draping Ginny's forgotten stole around her shoulders as they left. 'And the next time you speak to your friend Libby, you can tell her that her future uncle Bernard says that, even with only her uncle Michael to judge by, hers is a family worth having.'

'I think Libby already knows that,' sighed Ginny, as they followed Michael and Francine into the foyer. 'And once she and Jean-Claude are. . . Good heavens, look at that lightning!' she gasped, as the street beyond the plate glass façade took on a momentary appearance of broad daylight.

'Ah, the bliss of rain,' exclaimed Bernard, as the other two joined them.

'Great, isn't it?' grinned Michael. 'I've asked them

to bring our cars round—in fact, here they are.' He took Ginny by the arm and led her outside, and all four of them stood in the covered walkway taking deep gulps of rain-freshened air.

They made their farewells, Bernard kissing Ginny on both cheeks; Francine kissing Michael full on the mouth and receiving a muttered rebuke from her uncle for having done so.

'Drive carefully,' warned Bernard, as Michael started up the engine. 'And I'll contact you once I have that information we discussed.'

Ginny sat huddled and tense as they drove off, feeling the finality of their aloneness and the ominous silence accompanying it bearing down on her like a crushing weight.

'I guess you'll just have to save all that cosy chit-chat you were planning on till we get home,' muttered Michael, increasing the speed of the windscreen-wipers as he peered out through the torrents buffeting the car. 'I'll be too busy getting us through this lot to be my usual scintillating company.'

Ginny didn't bother acknowledging his words; she was too preoccupied with the depressing question of when, if ever, life would be normal again.

CHAPTER NINE

THE rain had let up a good deal by the time they reached the villa, but they still had to race from the car indoors to avoid getting drenched.

'Now we can have that cosy little chat,' announced Michael, scowling down at Ginny in the hallway as she stood poised to race up the stairs to her room.

'It's late and I'm tired,' she stated woodenly.

'I'll do my best to keep it brief.'

His peremptory tone sent anger scudding through Ginny's exhaustion. 'Let me put it another way,' she said. 'I don't want to speak to you. In fact, I'd consider it a blessing if I never had to speak another word to you again.'

'You spend a night in a guy's arms, then tell him a couple of days later you don't even want to speak to him again,' he drawled, 'and you reckon that's normal behaviour?'

'You can think what you like about my behaviour,' she retorted flatly, 'but yours in unspeakable!'

'Unspeakable, is it?' he enquired, shrugging out of his jacket. 'Come on and I'll make us some coffee and we can try to put this unspeakable behaviour of mine into some sort of language.'

'I don't want coffee.'

'OK, tea, cocoa, alcohol—take your pick, but we're going to talk.' He hung his jacket over the top of the balustrade, giving her a cold, humourless smile as he did so. 'We've been here before, Ginny, so save us both some time and accept right now that we *are* going to talk.'

'I accept that bullies always win,' she retorted angrily, and marched ahead of him into the kitchen.

She sat down at the kitchen table, placed her elbows on it and her chin on her hands. When her stole slid from her shoulders she made no attempt to retrieve it; she just sat there, numb with fatigue and wide open to the host of miseries besetting her.

He brought a jug of lemonade and two glasses to the table.

'What message was it you forgot to pass on to Libby from Bernard?' he demanded abruptly.

'God, I don't believe this!' she groaned. 'That the guns she's buying for her group of terrorists are ready for shipment! I simply forgot to tell her that he'd called, for heaven's sake. Look—I'm sick and tired of trying to convince you that Libby's all right. I'm obviously never going to succeed, so why don't you just leave me alone to wallow in self-pity—which is the only thing I'm up to at the moment!'

Her chin nearly skidded off her hands with surprise as he responded with a weary chuckle. She glowered across the table at him as he began pouring the lemonade. He had rolled up the sleeves of his dress-shirt, the white of the material contrasting dazzlingly with the silken blackness of the hairs on his deeply tanned arms—strong arms that had once held her in the mindless bliss of passion. She gave a shake of her head, again almost dislodging her chin from its perch. No wonder all she wanted to do was wallow in self-pity—she was obsessed!

'Ginny, don't you think I'm also entitled to a bit of self-pity?' he asked.

Her eyes met his in surprise, widening in shock as

they saw how drawn he looked, then hardening as she angrily told herself it was only an illusion created by the shadow of an incipient beard.

'Obviously you don't,' he muttered. 'But I reckon I am. The bottom line is I've no way of knowing to what extent your behaviour towards me relates to Libby.' He held up a hand to silence her as she made to speak. 'OK, so you're sick and tired of having you tell me that over and over when it's as plain as daylight that something's not right. But I have no idea how bad things might be—all I have is you to go by and you're worse than useless to me—far worse.'

'I suppose you mean that, unlike that other friend of Libby's you seduced, I didn't oblige by coming up with the information you were after,' burst out Ginny accusingly.

'If I were you, I'd be very careful how I interpreted any third-hand stories I'd heard about how information was allegedly obtained from that somewhat untypical friend of Libby's,' he warned her in icy tones. 'Apart from anything else, I, unlike you, have no stomach for the idea of sex being used as a weapon.'

'Unlike me?' Ginny almost howled at him in outrage.

'What am I supposed to think?' he demanded harshly. 'I'm the one in the dark, remember? What's to stop me thinking you spent a night with me in the hope you'd have me eating out of your hand afterwards? Certainly not your behaviour since.'

'You're sick!' whispered Ginny, appalled. 'You're twisting everything.'

'Am I?' he demanded coldly. 'And it's just my imagination—or perhaps my ego—that tells me you still want me as much as I want you?'

'No! I. . .Whether I want you or not has nothing to do with it,' she choked.

'To me it has one hell of a lot to do with it,' he said, his tone bordering on indifferent, despite his claim. 'Being a fairly simple guy, I begin to wonder how come you can give in to what you want one day and subject yourself to all this resistance the next.'

'Yes, you're so simple it wouldn't occur to you that I might object to playing musical beds with you and your other women!' lashed out Ginny in disgust. 'Though I'm not really being fair to you, am I, you revolting hypocrite? I wasn't supposed to know what was going on. I'm sure Aurelie wasn't aware that your bed was still barely cold from me when—'

'Aurelie?' he exploded, glaring at her in disbelief. 'Are you out of your mind? I've never—'

'Save your breath, Michael,' she cut in scathingly. 'Those hypocritical remarks you trot out with such ease simply won't work.'

'With you I trot out nothing with any ease,' he snapped, shaking his head. 'Hell, you're probably right—you and I would be a darned sight better off if we never exchanged another word. My God—Aurelie!' He dragged his fingers exasperatedly through his hair. 'To you, all this has been about me getting you back into my bed—don't you hear anything I'm saying to you, for God's sake?'

Ginny rose to her feet, her face a mask of tight coldness.

He glanced up at her, shaking his head. 'No—now isn't the time to walk away, Ginny,' he warned grimly. 'You don't accuse a man of what you've just accused me, then get up and walk away without hearing what he has to say.'

'There you go again, twisting everything,' she accused witheringly, hating him.

'For God's sake, Ginny, grow up,' he snapped. 'Just what sort of guy do you think I am? I don't know what you were doing prowling around the place in the middle of the night, as you plainly were the night Aurelie arrived, but if you'd taken the trouble to hang around a few seconds after seeing her go into my room, you'd have seen her come straight back out.'

'I—I didn't see her going into your room,' stammered Ginny, the impact of his words sending her sinking back down on to the chair. 'She was coming out.'

'In or out,' he barked impatiently, 'it was only a matter of seconds between them.'

'And now I suppose you're going to tell me she'd lost her way in the dark,' retorted Ginny, shock lending belligerence to her words.

He gave her a slightly startled look, then dragged his fingers through his hair once more, this time in a gesture almost of embarrassment. 'I guess I am,' he muttered.

'Or perhaps she decided to have a go at propositioning you in the middle of the night and you, lily-white saint that you are, sent her packing?' The accusing words appeared from nowhere, making her cringe even as she uttered them.

His look startled her with its sudden coldness.

'Why not just accept that she got confused in a strange place?' he suggested icily.

Ginny closed her eyes as she felt her head start to spin. There were a lot of things making her feel wobbly, one of them being an unshakeable certainty that he had been telling her the truth and was now lying—a lie born of a chivalry that threw her completely. Propositioning her boss in the middle of the night was something she had no difficulty seeing the bubbly, zany Aurelie undertaking, and without a qualm if the mood so took her.

'All right,' she muttered awkwardly, 'I accept it.' Her heart executed an unsteady flip when she saw the relief her words brought to his eyes. 'And I'm sorry for thinking otherwise.'

'Apology accepted,' he muttered, folding his arms on the table and gazing up at her as he rested his chin on them. 'And I guess perhaps I owe you an apology or two,' he continued pensively, but his eyes were wary, almost accusing. 'Though you didn't do anything to try to make a case for yourself over the business of that married guy—the opposite, in fact.'

'And you'd have believed me, would you?' she asked wearily, her mind only half on the subject as it kept slipping away to examine the truth about Aurelie's stay and to wonder how things might have been had she not leapt to such a devastating conclusion.

'You believed me just now, didn't you?' he countered. 'Anyway, it was wrong of me to put it to you as I did—it was no more than an unsubstantiated rumour.'

'You mean it was a rumour supplied by my aunt and substantiated by nobody else in the village,' sighed Ginny, with more wryness than bitterness.

'I really couldn't say,' he responded uneasily, then expanded slightly. 'It was a pretty sketchy report altogether.'

'And, for your records, completely untrue as far as any participation on my part was concerned. But there's no need for you to try to protect me from anything my aunt might have said about me—I don't have any illusions about her attitude towards me,' said Ginny, while frustratedly telling herself that her being wrong about Aurelie was no reason for the huge waves of love that kept threatening to drown her—nothing had actually changed.

'Neither should you have any illusions about me trying to protect you from anything,' he retorted sharply, his look startlingly hostile as he glanced over at her. 'It's time you were in your bed, you look tired.'

Feeling peculiarly nonplussed, Ginny rose to her feet. 'Maybe that's why I'm having such a problem working out what it was you insisted I came in here to hear,' she puzzled artlessly, while realising that something had indeed changed. Her only decent weapon against loving him had gone.

'Maybe I only got around to saying part of it,' he sighed, rising. He picked up her stole and draped it almost absent-mindedly around her. 'I've got some thinking to do about a few things—such as whether your remaining here serves any purpose at all.'

She reeled back as though he had hit her. 'No doubt you'll inform me when you've reached your decision,' she stated hoarsely, then turned and walked from the room.

She was halfway up the staircase when she heard a muffled roar from the kitchen. Seconds later he was beside her.

'How come every time you're in doubt, you interpret what I say at the lowest level of negativity you possibly can?' he demanded angrily.

'I'd need an exceptionally vivid imagination to find anything in the least positive in being told I serve no useful purpose here,' she retorted frigidly, her eyes trained resolutely ahead of her as she finished climbing the stairs and turned down the corridor. 'I was under the impression I was employed here to cook and tend the—'

'And I was under the impression you couldn't wait to get away from here,' he exploded through her words.

'And you were perfectly right,' she flung at him as they arrived at the door of her room.

'So how come you're objecting now that I'm considering letting you go?'

'I'm *not* objecting to that!' she howled in fury. 'I'm objecting to being described as useless.'

'Damn you, Ginny, stop making this up as you go along,' he accused. 'I didn't describe you as useless. 'What I said was. . .' He broke off and flung his hands in the air in exasperation. 'I said and you said and he said and she said,' he chanted dismissively. 'In the end, what difference does it make?' He reached out and took both her hands in his. 'Sleep well, Ginny,' he said with a wry smile, then leaned forward and kissed her on the cheek.

It was in the instant that his lips met the smoothness of her cheek that a small sound escaped her and his body tensed suddenly.

'Now, that wasn't such a clever idea, was it?' he whispered hoarsely, his breath soft against her cheek.

'No, it wasn't,' she agreed unquestioningly, as fire swept through her. 'What wasn't?' she asked unsteadily.

'This wasn't,' he groaned. 'Ginny, if I let go of your hands, you could use them to push me away.'

'Yes.'

He let go of her hands.

'You're not pushing me away,' he said, no trace of censure in his tone.

'No.'

'Are you going to?'

'No.'

'But you know what this is doing to me.'

'Yes.'

'And what's that, Ginny?'

'The same thing as it's doing to me.'

When his lips began nuzzling against her cheek, Ginny closed her eyes and tried to ask herself what she was doing. At first she had difficulty concentrating on that question, but it was the beautiful, melting madness seeping softly through her that eventually answered it—she was giving in to love.

'There's still time to push me away,' he insisted, a hot moistness in his breath as it feathered against her cheek.

'That's called passing the buck,' she shivered, but gave a gasp of shock as he took her by the shoulders, his fingers biting sharply into her flesh.

'No,' he protested, a glittering brightness in the eyes drilling down into hers. 'I want you so much I need you to be. . .' His words deteriorated into a ragged gasp as she reached out and rested her arms around his waist, and then something exploded between them.

It was to his room that he eventually carried her; a slow tortuous journey, interrupted time and again by hot, clinging kisses and frantic struggles to shed clothing. She was so lost in the heady intoxication of being in the only place she wanted to be that had he torn her treasured dress to ribbons in removing it from her, she would barely have noticed. But he didn't: with a breathless, trembling gentleness he removed every shred she wore while his softly incoherent murmurings filled her with a piercing ache of love.

He laughed at her guileless impatience as she tried to hurry his undressing, soft laughter that was filled with pleasure. But when he at last drew her down beside him on the bed, his attempts to temper the ferocity of the need consuming him found no co-operation in the tense, eager body laying blatant siege to his.

'What are you doing to me?' he groaned in the moment before he gave in with an explosive cry of exultation.

The first shock that rippled through her was one of ecstatic recognition. Part of her had begun to believe that her memory had deceived her, but now she knew that no memory could possibly have held intact the wonder that had happened to her before and was happening to her all over again. She cried out in joyous welcome to those innumerable buds of sensation erupting within her, abandoning herself to them as they swelled and filled her to over-brimming with the never-ending bombardments of pleasure into which each exploded. When she tried to speak, they smothered her words with the power of their indescribable intensity. But when the final, obliterating explosion possessed them both in a wild orgy of ecstatic sensation, the words being smothered in her were words of love.

It was the knowledge that she could so easily have cried out her love that jarred through the lazy, beautiful cloud on which she was floating, bringing her back to reality with a brutality that flung her to the brink of depression.

'Do you know what?' he murmured lazily, sliding down the bed till his head was cushioned against her breasts.

'What?' she whispered, an overwhelming surge of love drawing her back from that brink as she cradled him to her.

'I'm at a loss for words. . . So I guess I might just as well shut up.'

She ran the fingers of one hand lightly through his hair and caressed his back with the other, the dark sadness still swirling within her unable to dilute her love.

'Up a bit,' he joked lazily, twitching a shoulder, 'and a little to the left.'

'I thought you'd decided to shut up,' she teased softly, feeling her heart would burst.

'I think I'd better—I exhausted my last drop of energy moving my shoulder just then,' he chuckled.

Lying with his arms around her and hers around him was almost like being part of him, and several times she detected barely perceptible indications that he was about to speak. But each time it happened the moment passed without his uttering a single word, and gradually she felt herself fill with resentment; not towards the silent man in whose arms she lay, but towards the girl she had always loved as a sister. She couldn't go on like this, not telling him the truth—she simply couldn't. But first she had to tell Libby everything and warn her what she was about to do.

Feeling as though a tiny part of her burden had already been removed from her, she dropped a kiss on the dark head nestling against her.

'So—you are awake,' he murmured with a lazy chuckle, raising his head to gaze down at her.

'I haven't been——' She broke off with an involuntary gasp as desire surged hotly in his body, instantly infecting her own with its potent urgency.

'This time we're playing by my rules,' he informed her huskily, his fingers teasing against her already tensely swollen breasts, then moving tantalisingly down her body, 'so be warned.'

To her it seemed like hours, though it was probably only minutes, before she broke beneath the maddening, exquisitely pleasurable ministrations of the hands and mouth laying siege to her exquisitely aroused body. It seemed like several hours more before, in desperation, she retaliated with like for like and was rewarded with a surrender that swept her up and carried her away to a world of incomparable fulfilment.

Ginny peered down at the coffee-jug in her hands, frowning at the sight of the unground coffee-beans over which she had just poured water.

She moved to the sink, poured off the water and discarded the beans. She shook her head, trying to clear it of the mind-blowing memories of the night before that, without warning, kept blasting through it and destroying her ability to reason. Why didn't Libby call? She couldn't go on like this for much longer, she told herself frantically, she *had* to tell Michael the truth. He was waiting for her to tell him, silently, urgently willing her with an intensity that was almost tangible.

Blinking back the threat of tears, she measured coffee, this time ground, into the jug. Or perhaps she was simply imagining that he was, she vacillated edgily as she thought of him as he had been all day. In a manner completely at odds with his forceful personality, Michael was behaving in a way that could only be described as withdrawn.

Apprehension shuddered through her; perhaps his behaviour was more to do with the fact that his involvement, unlike hers, was exclusively physical. Had it not been for the still-insatiable need that had ignited without warning several times already during the day, she was beginning to have the terrible feeling that he would have withdrawn from her completely—that he inevitably would once his physical need for her had burned itself out.

She took several shuddering breaths to steady herself, then glanced up suddenly, alerted by a built-in antenna, her heart already lurching in a drunken explosion of love even before Michael walked through the doorway.

'I'm just making coffee,' she said, busying herself with putting on more water as she battled for composure.

'Good—we can——' He broke off and reached for the telephone ringing on the wall beside him.

Ginny felt her pulses pound with alarm. If it was Libby, she would just have to hope he would leave the room, as he had that last time, when she spoke to her.

'Yes, thanks for getting back to me, Bernard,' he said, the discovery that it wasn't Libby making Ginny's pulses pound even harder with disappointment. 'Yes, I've already got someone working on it. . . No, look, I'll explain when I see you—I've had enough of being messed about. . . No, I'll be on my own.'

Ginny's hands were shaking uncontrollably as she got down the cups and saucers. She hadn't bargained for love doing this to her, but whereas her heart had pounded at the idea of what she would have to say to Libby, it was now hammering out of control because of what she had just overheard.

'That was Bernard,' he said, when she finally got herself enough in control to carry their coffee to the table.

'Yes,' she said, slopping half her own coffee into its saucer. She hesitated for a couple of seconds before the fear burst from her. 'Michael, please don't do anything foolish. . . You've managed this long, so—'

'Foolish?' he demanded, tight-lipped with fury. 'I've *managed*, have I, Ginny?' With an angry swipe of his hand he sent the cup and saucer she had just placed before him flying across the room. 'No, Ginny, I haven't managed, it's been eating away inside me. And I haven't been foolish—I've been plain out of my mind.' He rose to his feet, kicking aside his chair as he did so. 'I've tried everything I can think of with you, but now I'm through. I'm going out—and I want you out of here by the morning!'

It was a long time before Ginny's besieged mind could let go of its conviction that it was the business of the thefts from their companies to which Michael had been referring when he had spoken to Bernard, and by then he had been gone for some time.

She gave a shiver of horror as she at last accepted it must have been Libby he was referring to, then buried her face in her hands as it dawned on her how her own pleading words must have sounded to this already-suspicious mind. She hadn't even a number on which to contact Libby, she thought frustratedly, then rose to her feet, deciding that later she would look to see if she could find an address book or diary in Libby's room.

She gazed around her, an empty, brittle calm creeping over her and switching her mind on to hold. She took her own cup and saucer to the sink and washed them up. Then she cleared the floor of the smashed remnants of the other cup and saucer and wiped the splashes that had reached as far as one of the walls. Even when she felt the inherent violence in those dark, ragged streaks marring the whitewashed purity of the wall reach out to threaten her, her deceptively fragile calm fought back and remained intact.

Later, when she had searched Libby's room in vain for Jeanne's number, she felt the first crack in that protective veneer; then the telephone began ringing and a tiny sliver of relief got through to her as she flew to answer it.

'Miss Price? Ginny?' enquired an English voice that she recognised as once having been instantly familiar to her, but which now only managed to ring a distant bell in the far reaches of her memory. 'Howard Johnston here.'

'Mr Johnston—from the bank?' she asked, disappointment draining her.

'The very one, my dear,' replied the voice, a hint of strain in its heartiness.

'How on earth did you get this number?' Ginny croaked.

'With considerable difficulty, I'm afraid. There was no mention of the name of the owner of the property you left as a forwarding address. Even once we traced the name, getting the telephone number was something of a battle.'

'Oh, I am sorry. But thank you for forwarding my mail, Mr Johnston, it was so kind of you to agree to do so in the first place and——' Ginny broke off as reason pulled her up sharply. 'Mr Johnston, why are you ringing me here?'

'It's to do with your aunt—Miss Bond,' he stated gently. 'Ginny, I'm afraid she's had a pretty massive stroke. John Maynard, the doctor, asked if I could get in touch with you. . . Ginny, are you still there?'

'Yes, Mr Johnston, I'm still here,' she answered faintly. 'And thank you very much for contacting me—I'll be back as soon as I possibly can.'

She wondered dazedly why she was crying. She had been too frozen by the callousness of Michael's words and his leaving to be capable of tears over him—though she knew they must come—but in her heart of hearts she knew she had no honest tears for the aunt whose treatment of her, over the years, had been unfeeling, if not downright cruel. Perhaps it was the gentle caring that had been in the bank manager's voice—a man who had known her since her fateful tenth year and who, like so many others in the village, had shown her innumerable small kindnesses, as though trying in some measure to make up for what her aunt so patently lacked.

At least she no longer had the problem of nowhere to go to contend with—now her problem was one of finding a fare back to England that wouldn't deplete the kitty by too much.

She was far too early for the bus that would take her to the airport. She had time and again to check and recheck her passport, tickets and luggage, until awareness of an element of obsessiveness in her actions sent her mind veering off in search of something else to occupy it.

The trouble was that her mind was drained from a night of constant activity. Throughout those sleepless hours there had been a part of her on constant alert for Michael's return. Another part had been preoccupied with guilt: guilt over abandoning Libby and guilt over the ambivalence of her feelings over the news about her aunt, until the memories of her childhood, stirring like an evil darkness in her soul, had put paid to much of that particular guilt. And then, there had been Michael; all trace of the guilt she had once felt, every counterfeit moment of tenderness she had deluded herself into believing they had shared, gone—erased by the callousness with which he had dismissed her. No matter how much she had craved to believe it to be otherwise, it was obvious it had been nothing more than cold calculation that had governed his every action towards her.

She gave an angry toss of her head to clear it from the agonies of the night. Even waiting for the bus in the village for the best part of an hour had to be better than hanging around here going slowly out of her mind, she informed herself harshly, and gathered her things together.

She closed the front door behind her, bitterness and desolation washing over her in huge waves. When she turned towards the drive and saw first Michael's car, and then Michael himself emerging from it, rumpled and with a scowling, unshaven face, she had no difficulty convincing herself that it was her imagination playing a horrible trick on her, and she made her way down the steps to the drive.

'Ginny, just what the hell do you think you're doing?' he rasped, his eyes screwing up against the brightness of the early morning sun as he raked impatient fingers through his dishevelled hair.

All right, so it wasn't her imagination, she told herself, her mouth clamping into a tight line as she hooked one of her bags more securely over her shoulder. But he was the past, and the past was over and done with—there was nothing she had to say to him.

'Ginny!' he bellowed irritably, striding towards her as she walked steadily on down the drive. 'Damn it, Ginny, you can't just walk out like this—I didn't mean what I said yesterday.'

He had said one or two things yesterday, she thought

with an almost careless detachment—which one of them was he now claiming not to have meant?

'Ginny, this is crazy,' he exclaimed, walking backwards in front of her as she marched determinedly on. 'We have to talk.'

'I have a plane to catch,' she stated woodenly.

'For God's sake, you can't just run off like this,' he protested, his frown, as he saw the ravaged pallor of her face, deepening with alarm as he caught sight of the blank detachment dulling the life from her eyes. 'Ginny, if you're really determined to go,' he said quietly, 'won't you at least let me drive you to the airport?'

'No!' she exploded, then bit viciously on her bottom lip as an alien something struggled to break free within her. 'I couldn't bear to have to breathe the same air as you!'

'For God's sake, Ginny——'

'No—that's not what I meant! I deserve what you did to me. . . You'll never know what a wicked person I am—how I deserve far worse than anything you could ever do to me!'

'Ginny, what in God's name are you saying?' he rasped, coming to an abrupt halt.

She walked on, and when she reached the end of the drive the only movement he had made was to turn to gaze after her, a look of bemused horror on his face.

CHAPTER TEN

'It was very kind of you to come round, Mr Beresford,' said Ginny, a look of brooding preoccupation on her face as she escorted her late aunt's elderly solicitor to the door of John and Mary Maynard's cottage. 'I can't begin to tell you how much I appreciate all you've told me.'

And she honestly couldn't, thought Ginny dazedly, leaning back against the door after closing it behind him.

She remained motionless, the coldness from the blast of winter air to which she had been so briefly subjected lingering on her cheeks, while a comforting warmth spread healingly through her. In the week since her return to England there had been times when she had been almost overwhelmed by the spontaneous gestures of kindness and understanding offered her by the people of the village—a place she had never been able to bring herself to think of as home—some, people she recognised yet barely knew, others, like the doctor, John Maynard, and his wife Mary, with whom she had been relatively friendly but had not kept in touch with once she had left.

She closed her eyes, the realisation prickling through her of how close she had been to collapse that day she had arrived back and learned of her aunt's death. And it had been Mary and John, brushing aside all her incoherent protestations, who had insisted she stay with them rather than in the cold, empty house in which she had spent so many unhappy years.

'Ginny, are you OK?' asked Mary, anxiety clouding her attractive face as she appeared at the kitchen door.

Ginny's eyes flew open. 'I'm more than OK,' she announced with a reassuring smile. 'I'm just trying to collect my thoughts. I can't say I was particularly looking forward to Mr Beresford's visit, but in retrospect, I wouldn't have missed it for the world.'

'I've just made some tea,' said Mary, giving her a slightly puzzled look before disappearing back into the kitchen. 'I'll bring it into there,' she called, and joined Ginny moments later in the bright, chintzy living-room. She placed a tea-tray on the table beside the sofa. 'So, you wouldn't have missed Mr B's visit for the world,' she murmured, her tone half-questioning.

'I wouldn't,' confirmed Ginny. 'He told me so many things I needed to know.'

'Including why your aunt excluded you from her will?'

Ginny shook her head. 'Mary, I can't understand why everyone's so shocked about that,' she sighed. 'But I promise you, I'd have keeled over with shock if she'd left me so much as a halfpenny.'

'Perhaps, but to leave everything to some obscure charity and you without a roof over your head,' protested Mary, handing her a cup.

'And that's all it ever was,' exclaimed Ginny with a grimace, 'a roof over my head—I hated the place.' She took a sip from her cup, her expression lightening. 'No—what Mr Beresford told me was worth far more to me than a dozen roofs over my head. Until today, I'd no idea he and his wife were contemporaries of my grandparents.' She broke off and gave a small, disbelieving shake of her head. 'It still hasn't sunk in properly—so many things I'd no idea of,' she mused, almost to herself. 'The times I used to look at Aunt

Irene, and then think of my mother. . . I was never able to come to terms with the idea of someone so unlike my mother, someone so completely without warmth and love, being her flesh and blood—my own, too.'

Mary flashed her a troubled look. 'Ginny, it really doesn't pay to think along such lines. Sometimes in families——'

'But she *wasn't* family,' cut in Ginny with sudden animation. 'I'd never have known if it hadn't been for Mr Beresford. My grandparents adopted her when she was very young—her parents, with whom they'd been friendly, had died suddenly and very young.'

'And she never got over their death?' asked Mary.

Ginny shook her head. 'According to Mr Beresford, it wasn't like that at all. She was very happy with my grandparents and she particularly adored my grandmother. They were a very happy family.'

'Until your mother came along,' sighed Mary. 'What age would your aunt have been then?'

'Fifteen,' replied Ginny. 'And it wasn't so much my mother's arrival that upset her as the fact that the birth left my grandmother a semi-invalid—she was in her late forties when she had my mother.'

'So it wasn't just you—she made life hell for your poor mother too,' gasped Mary.

'No, Mr Beresford says my grandparents were far too intelligent and well-adjusted to have allowed even a breath of anything like that into their lives. He says that Irene had always been an introverted, rather obssessive child, but it was only when my grandmother died that she really turned against my mother—holding her ultimately responsible for my grandmother's death.'

'But what age was your poor mother?'

'Sixteen,' sighed Ginny. 'And still struggling to come to terms with her father's death, which had happened less than a year before—though Irene had coped with that fairly well. Mr Beresford told me that my grandmother had admitted to his wife that she had a premonition she wouldn't outlive my grandfather by very long.'

Mary took a drink from her cup, her expression pensive. 'It's a pity no one thought to tell you all this years ago,' she exclaimed exasperatedly. 'Ginny, I know John and I are relative newcomers, but we'd be blind not to notice there's quite a bit of collective guilt in this place concerning the way your aunt treated you. A lot of it surfaced when you left so suddenly. . . And you'd probably be surprised to learn of the number of people who rounded on her—and quite vociferously—when it got out why you'd gone.'

'I've learned a lot in this past week,' said Ginny, a harsh tremor running through her as something that had lain mercifully dormant during that time stirred threateningly within her. 'One thing being that I should have stayed and faced up to my aunt and the lies that creep I worked for told her.'

'Ginny, you mustn't start thinking your staying would have changed anything,' exclaimed Mary, horrified.

'No—I wasn't thinking that at all,' Ginny assured her, then added hesitantly, 'But for a while I felt I must be some sort of monster. . .feeling practically nothing when Mr Johnston rang me and told me. . . And then, when I heard she'd died, feeling only guilt over not feeling anything.'

'For heaven's sake, Ginny, how could you possibly expect to feel anything for a woman who, from what I can gather, treated you without a shred of compassion?' groaned Mary. 'My God, I've never seen anyone so close to breaking point as you were that day you came back!'

'That had very little to do with my aunt,' protested Ginny guiltily, all those temporarily suppressed feelings now rising like a bitter bile in her. 'I'd made a complete fool of myself over a man who, to be blunt, had used me. . . It had got to a stage where I was beginning to believe I'd become that ghastly person my aunt always said I was.'

'Ginny, it sounds to me as though you could do with some counselling,' stated Mary anxiously. 'John would be only too happy to arrange it for you.'

'If it hadn't been for Mr Beresford's visit, I think I'd have taken you up on that,' said Ginny. 'I realise what a state I was in when I arrived, but that had a lot to do with a deep-down fear I had of ending up as bitter and twisted as my aunt was. . . It may sound completely irrational to you, but that's why what Mr Beresford told me meant so much to me—it was like being set free.'

'That doesn't sound in the least irrational to me,' murmured Mary, reaching over and patting her hand. 'And it probably won't come as much consolation to you, but I came pretty close to cracking up over a rat of a man shortly before I met John—and now I can barely remember what the creep looked like.'

She rose and stacked the tray, her eyes clouding as they saw the look of utter desolation flit across Ginny's face.

'Ginny, I don't know what your plans are, but you're welcome to stay here indefinitely—you do know that, don't you?'

Ginny nodded, forcing a smile to her lips as she

tried in vain to clear her head of the memories rampaging through it.

'I know you're worried about your friend,' continued Mary gently, 'and that's understandable. But if returning to France entails running into this man again, I'd think twice, if I were you—you've obviously still quite a bit of recovering to do where he's concerned.'

A lifetime of it, thought Ginny wretchedly, rising to her feet and picking up the tray Mary had been about to lift.

'Perhaps my luck will change and someone like your John will turn up,' she called with forced lightness over her shoulder as she carried the tray into the kitchen.

'Actually, he has got this rather hunky friend,' teased Mary, following after her. 'I could always——'

'Mrs Maynard,' interrupted Ginny with joking primness, 'aren't you supposed to be standing in for the surgery receptionist this afternoon?'

Mary pulled a face and gave a theatrical shiver. 'It's freezing outside,' she protested, then glanced at her watch. 'Though I suppose I should be getting a move on,' she sighed. 'But that won't stop me doing a bit of plotting and planning while I shunt the patients through,' she added with a chuckle. 'Oh, by the way, I forgot to tell you—someone from the bank dropped round a couple of letters for you earlier. They're on the table in the hall.'

Once Mary had gone, Ginny collected the two envelopes from the hall. She took them back into the living-room and sat down, her gaze fixing sightlessly on them while her mind dipped recklessly in and out of memories she feared would continue to plague her till the day she died. Barely conscious of the scalding wetness of the tears trickling slowly down her cheeks, she began prising open the first of the envelopes on her lap. She gave a soft groan of disbelief as, through blurred eyes, she made out a bank statement informing her of the princely sum of eighty-seven pence in her account. She tossed the statement aside in a gesture of despair—she didn't need reminding that the problem of her penury was one she would have to address with urgency. Her shoulders sagging, she went through the motions of opening the second envelope. The sheet of paper she drew out lay folded in her hand as she leaned back and closed her eyes, her thoughts running free. Mary had suggested counselling, she thought numbly, but no amount of counselling could ever bring her to terms with what Michael had done to her. Nothing could ever explain to her how two bodies could join in such exquisite passion, one driven by love and the other by. . . A shudder racked through her; he had wanted her, but he had wanted what she knew about Libby far more.

Trembling, she forced her attention back to the paper in her hand. Her eyes widened, as she read, her head shaking from side to side in disbelief. Her sole legacy from her parents had been the Premium Bonds they had bought her on her first birthday. Even had the one hundred pounds they were worth been all that lay between her and destitution, she would never have been able to bring herself to cash them in—and now one of them had won her the unbelievable sum of five thousand pounds!

She was still shaking her head and clutching the notification, when the ring of the doorbell brought her to her feet. The ghost of an affectionate smile creeping to her lips, she scrubbed away any last trace of tears and went to the door. Mary was always forgetting something—this time it appeared to be her keys.

'You'll never believe. . . No!' She shrank back, that

final denial bursting from her in a ragged croak of horror.

She found herself gripping the door, hanging on to it for support while her mind spontaneously emptied itself in order to accommodate the suddenly vital question of what it was that seemed so disconcertingly unfamiliar about the man before her. It wasn't the expression of grim harshness on those devastatingly attractive features—that was an expression she knew only too well. Nor was it those eyes clear and as falsely true-blue honest as they always had been.

'No? Does that mean you're not about to let me in?' he asked, the soft, familiar American cadences in his voice ripping open a thousand wounds in her. 'It's very damp and cold out here.'

That was what was so different about him—his clothes. She was used to seeing him in the casual elegance of lightweight clothing. Now he was dressed to accommodate the harshness of an English winter, a long dark coat, faultlessly tailored, its collar dragged up to shield his neck from a rain-laden wind.

'OK, if you don't feel happy about talking here——'

'What are you doing here?' she blurted out, her mind, its initial problem solved, retreating into blankness. 'How did you find this——?'

'Damn it, Ginny, I have a hire car parked over the road,' he snapped impatiently. 'We can talk there if you're not about to let me in.'

She hesitated, then opened the door wider and let him in.

'Libby gave me the address you used to live at,' he muttered. 'It was a neighbour who told me you were staying here.'

'Libby?' croaked Ginny.

'Yes, Libby,' he replied, and shrugged off his coat

to reveal a heavy, roll-neck sweater in dark charcoal grey and immaculately cut trousers in an even darker hue.

There was something slightly saturnine in his dark-clad appearance, thought Ginny almost abstractedly, then pulled herself up sharply and took the coat from him as he began looking around him for somewhere to hang it. She felt the luxurious sensation of cashmere beneath her hands and the subtle masculine scent of him envelop her, heightening her half-dream state and sending hot shafts of an unbearable longing coursing through her as she hung the coat up in the hall cupboard.

'Libby,' she repeated dazedly, closing the cupboard door and leaning heavily against it, shaken by the ungovernable strength of the need pounding through her and horrified by the fact that, though several questions were trying to form in her mind, not one of them could she assemble into words.

'Libby's fine,' he muttered in a hoarse, peculiarly hollow voice. 'She——' He broke off, then glanced almost bemusedly around him, his tall, broad-shouldered presence somehow shrinking the generous proportions of the hall. 'Look, when I decided to come here, I'd no idea how things were for you. . . That neighbour I said I spoke to—she told me your aunt had died.'

He couldn't actually be saying he had seen Libby, she reasoned frantically, otherwise he would hardly describe her as being fine. Perhaps Libby had rung him and managed to put his mind at rest.

'Ginny, if I'd known——'

'I—I'll make some coffee, if you like,' stammered Ginny, the offer blurting from her before before she knew she was making it. The last thing she needed or wanted was his misplaced sympathy. 'The living-room's through there.'

'Ginny, I don't want coffee. . . All I want is to talk.' He dragged his fingers almost nervously through his hair. 'But I guess I'm being selfish—you must have so many other things on your mind right now.'

Ginny's eyes flashed towards his, then quickly away. She might have been in a state when she had first arrived back, she thought hopelessly, but that was nothing to the way she was feeling now. Everything was crowding in on her, most of all love, draining the breath from her lungs as it stifled her with its unwanted, irrepressible presence.

'Yes, you are selfish, Michael,' she retorted, her words as vicious as the love persecuting her. 'But don't break a lifetime habit on my account.'

She swept past him and into the living-room.

He followed after her, silently waiting for her to be seated before selecting the armchair furthest from her for himself.

'Ginny, I. . . Hell, this doesn't seem right,' he exclaimed, his body stiff on the edge of the chair, as though ready to take flight.

'What doesn't seem right?'

'You just having had a death in your family and me assuming you'd want to hear about Libby and her husband and all the——'

'Her husband?' croaked Ginny, sitting bolt upright. 'What on earth are you saying?'

'Yeah, it sure has all been happening while you've been away,' he drawled in wearily derisive tones. 'The big event is being planned for after the baby's born, but the de Montoussés insisted on a quiet civil marriage right away—they weren't too enamoured of the idea of their first grandchild being born out of wedlock.'

'But Jean-Claude had been packed off to an oil rig,' protested Ginny weakly, shaking her swimming head in an attempt to clear it.

'Libby had already come to her senses and let him know how things were before I'd unearthed what was going on and contacted his parents,' he said. 'In fact, the pair of them arrived while I was with the parents.'

'Oh, poor Libby,' exclaimed Ginny, her head refusing to clear. 'Was Jean-Claude very upset she hadn't let him know? How did his parents react?' Frantic questions poured from her unchecked. 'Were they very annoyed? Poor Libby, she——'

'What's with all this poor Libby?' he cut in caustically. 'The whole scene was cotton candy schmaltz. The parents were all but swooning with delight at the thought of a grandchild, and for one terrible moment I thought they'd end up apologising for having been so hard on the love-birds. As for Jean-Claude's frame of mind, most of the time he and Libby gave the appearance of having been grafted together, so I guess he couldn't have been too upset.'

'I—I'm so happy for them,' whispered Ginny; or she would be, she vowed, once she had shaken off this terrible sensation of doom and desolation stifling her true feelings.

'Are you, Ginny?'

The effect of those drawlingly sceptical words was like a knife in her.

'Aren't you?' she exclaimed in disgust. 'The way you were carrying on, I'd have thought you'd be ecstatic.'

'I'm pleased they're OK—but ecstatic I'm not.' His expression hardened. 'Ginny, I know I got a lot of things wrong and that you were only being loyal to Libby. And I know she's right when she says it was only your inherent honesty making you act so guilty from the start. . . Hell, there were times when I was almost convinced it was that myself.' His eyes caught hers, a brooding, accusing darkness deepening their blue to navy as he slumped back heavily against the cushions. 'But there were all those other times, when you acted as though you were linked to a short-fused bomb—a bomb that finally went off the day you ran away.'

'I didn't run away—you ordered me to get out! Even if I hadn't had the news that my aunt wasn't well, I'd——'

'And how was I supposed to know about that?' he rasped. 'I'd spent the night trying to figure out what to do. Then, when I did try talking to you, you just freaked out on me. But I was the one nearly freaking out when you started saying how wicked you were. . . You surely can't blame me for assuming that this wickedness had something to do with Libby.'

Ginny gazed over at him in horror, her mouth opening but no sound escaping her.

'Damn it, what else could I think?' he demanded harshly. 'And even now, I can't make any sense of either that or what you said about the way I'd treated you.'

'Oh, Michael, I'm so sorry—so terribly sorry,' she whispered hoarsely. 'But that's all behind you now. . . You know Libby's all right and that's all that ever mattered to you. Why can't you accept that and be happy? Please. . . Why can't you just leave me alone?'

'I'm not happy—and I can't leave you alone,' he stated tonelessly.

She closed her eyes; she had yet to come to terms

with his actual presence, let alone statements such as the one he had just made.

'I—I'm sorry if you're not happy,' she stammered dazedly. 'But I'm glad everything has turned out all right for Libby. . . I was worried sick, having no means of contacting her to let her know why I'd left so suddenly.'

'Bernard and I managed to come up with a story to explain your disappearance,' he told her quietly. 'But she took a lot of persuading to go ahead with the wedding without you there.'

'What on earth did you tell her?'

'That you'd gone to England with Francine, because she wanted to buy a house there and needed someone English to hold her hand.' He gave a small shrug at her look of disbelief. 'Oh, Libby swallowed it, all right,' he assured her, 'especially when I explained that Francine was paying you handsomely for going—in fact, she got pretty tearful over that. . . Which reminds me,' he added, easing his lean-hipped body up in the chair and producing an envelope from his back pocket. 'Libby tried calling your old home number and got a dead line. She says to tell you she thought about writing, but there was so much to say that she said to tell you she's decided to keep it until you return to France.'

Most of what he was saying was making little sense to her, but Ginny found her mind incapable of working out just what was wrong with it, and her look was strained and perplexed as she eyed the envelope he was now holding in one hand and tapping absent-mindedly against the fingers of the other.

'No—she didn't change her mind about not writing,' he replied in answer to her unspoken question. 'It's a draft for the money you lent her.'

'It wasn't a loan,' protested Ginny unhappily. 'I—'

'Ginny, I know about your handing over every cent you possessed,' he countered quietly. 'If Libby hadn't told me, I wouldn't have been able to concoct such a convincing story for your absence.' He leaned over and placed the envelope on the low table between them.

'No—I don't need it,' she insisted, thoroughly distracted by the questions that kept floating half formed into her mind, only to slip away from her. 'I. . . But it was very kind of you to bring it to me.'

'I could have arranged to have it paid directly to your bank,' he pointed out, his eyes boring into her.

But he hadn't, thought Ginny wretchedly, then started visibly as a question at last clicked into place. 'If I'm supposed to be house-hunting with Francine, why on earth would Libby expect me to be here?' she asked.

'Because I told her you'd decided to stay on here a while after,' he replied.

'She'd never have believed you,' exclaimed Ginny, her feelings of unease and apprehension increasing with every passing second. 'What's happened? Are you telling me the truth about Libby?'

'I promise you, Libby and Jean-Claude have sailed off into the sunset and will probably live happily ever after,' he informed her with a bitter laugh. 'Though what happens to those caught in their wake is another matter. And you're right—Libby didn't believe me at first when I said you were staying on—until, that is, I let her know that things hadn't been as easy between us as you'd led her to believe.'

Ginny felt the colour drain from her face. 'Exactly what did you say to her?' she demanded hoarsely.

'Enough for her to order me straight over here and bring you back,' he replied.

'If you've a number for her, I'll ring her and speak to her,' she said huskily, then glanced down at the envelope on the table. 'But I honestly don't want that.'

'Ginny, however much your aunt may have left you doesn't figure in this—it's only right that you should be paid back.

'My aunt?' choked Ginny, then gave a croaked gasp of a laugh as something seemed to collapse within her. 'I'm the last person my aunt would have left anything to. I——' She broke off and leapt to her feet, panicked by an overwhelming premonition that everything within her was about to disintegrate. 'No. . . I—I'm sorry,' she gasped disjointedly, while her body acquiesced like a limp rag to the firm hands grasping her shoulders and pressing her down on to the sofa. 'I'd said all those terrible things to you about her,' she sobbed into the softness of cashmere against which her face had become pressed. 'And I felt hardly anything when I learned how ill she was. I *should* have loved her. . . I *would* have, if only she'd let me!'

'Ginny, love isn't an automatic right,' he stated firmly, gathering her to him, his body rocking hers in a gentle, soothing motion. 'It's something that often has to be earned, and that woman in no way ever earned any love from you. You were right when you thought I was trying to protect you over that report. . . But you knew anyway that any dirt must have come from her.'

'But she took me in! I wasn't even her flesh and blood, though I didn't know it till today. . . But she knew, and she still took me in!'

'And she still treated you badly,' he stated with stark

candour. 'And that's the bottom line. Right now, shock is distorting your ability to rationalise, but——'

'I know that,' protested Ginny, her efforts to pull herself together only awakening in her a throbbing awareness of being once more in his arms, and then the frantic need to escape it. She drew sharply away from him. 'I'm sorry,' she muttered, the need burning in her bringing a tremor to the hands impatiently rubbing the tears from her cheeks.

'Ginny, you're not the one who should be apologising,' he sighed heavily, moving quickly along the sofa to create further space between them.

'Yes, I am,' she insisted. 'You had no way of knowing what was going on in my mind the day I left. I honestly do realise that most of my guilts concerning my aunt are unfounded. But I didn't then. Then I felt I was being punished—that I deserved everything that had happened to me because of my wickedness in not caring. . . I was incapable of even contemplating how you might interpret such an outburst—and that was unforgivable.'

'No, it wasn't—but what you in fact said was that you deserved everything I'd done to you,' he stated tonelessly. 'Was my loving you such a terrible crime?'

For a brief moment an unbearable tension gripped her, only to leave her as she remembered Libby once declaring that American and English should be regarded as two separate languages. She was the one for whom loving and lovemaking had been one and the same thing—but it never had been for him.

'Yes—I guess it must have been,' he muttered, dragging his hands wearily over his face.

'Only because you made love to me for all the wrong reasons,' she informed him wearily. 'Perhaps that story about the way you used Libby's other friend was completely unfounded. . . But that's exactly how it felt you had used me.'

'Ginny, please,' he exclaimed hoarsely. 'Don't.'

'I'm just telling you how it felt,' she protested, great waves of hopelessness and desolation washing over her. 'You were so obsessed by Libby's non-appearance that it didn't even occur to you that when I heard you talking to Bernard over the phone I had thought you were talking about taking action over the thefts from your business.'

'What?' he exclaimed incredulously. 'It was Libby we were talking about! I told you the police were dealing——'

'I *know* that,' she protested. 'But at the time I got it into my head that you'd lost your patience and were going to do something stupid. It was only after you'd told me to get out and stormed off that I realised that I was the one with whom you'd lost patience.' She broke off with a weary shake of her head. 'There really isn't any point in going over all this—none whatsoever.'

'If you say so,' he shrugged, flashing her an oddly ambivalent look. 'But let's just get it straight. I didn't ask if making love to you was such a crime—I asked if *loving* you was.'

'You what?' croaked Ginny, and saw the room spin before her eyes.

'You're right—this is getting us nowhere,' he muttered, rising to his feet. 'There are just a couple of other things I wanted to tell you,' he added, his eyes avoiding hers, 'and then I'll go.'

'Michael——'

'The police got lucky: one of the thieves broke ranks and transferred some of the money back into the country—they arrested the whole group yesterday.'

'That's wonderful, but——'

'And the woman who took the money? That's all sorted too.'

'Michael——'

'The company dealing with her late husband's insurance kept giving her the runaround. The details are so tortuous they'd make your head reel, but when they eventually paid up they did so almost a month later than the date they'd promised. Her debts had been mounting and she had pledged settlement to coincide with the promised arrival date of the cheque. When it didn't show up on time, she panicked—the rest you know.'

'And she's still got her job,' said Ginny, the room now spinning wildly.

'She still has her job,' he confirmed, his eyes continuing to avoid hers. 'Plus a substantial additional sum she received in compensation from the insurers the day after I set my lawyers on them.'

'I. . .' She burst into tears before she could get any further.

'Ginny, don't,' he groaned, taking a hesitant step towards her, then freezing. 'Please don't. . . I thought you'd be pleased to hear——'

'I *am*!' she howled. 'This is nothing to do with that. Nothing's ever to do with what you think it is!'

'That figures,' he muttered hollowly.

'No—nothing figures!' she sobbed. 'Nothing about *you* figures! You talk about loving me—or, at least, that's what it sounded like to my befuddled mind—then you get up to go!'

'OK, you're befuddled—I'm plain insane,' he exclaimed wearily. 'Ginny, there was even a time I managed to delude myself that you felt the same way as I did.'

'Whatever makes you think you'd deluded yourself?' croaked Ginny, feeling as though she were suffocating.

He flashed her a startled look, then his jaw tensed. 'If you'd loved me, you'd have trusted me with any secret you had. Your loyalty to me would have superseded any you felt to Libby. You must have known how I felt about you and that I'd have done everything in my power to straighten things out for you.'

'Must I? Most of the time I felt you hated me. Not that that stopped me loving you, nor deciding I had to tell you everything. I'd already made up my mind to do that the day you told me to leave. The only thing that had prevented me doing so for a long time was Libby's pregnancy—she had become so vulnerable. I was praying she would ring, so that afterwards I could at last tell you the truth.'

'Ginny, I. . . Oh, hell—come here.' He was reaching out for her, even as she had begun to rise, hauling her up into his arms. 'I'm never going to recover from this,' he whispered distractedly, his arms tightening around her while his lips searched frantically against her face. 'Never in a million years! Have you any idea what you've done to me? I haven't been able to think straight since practically the day I met you.' He yanked her away from him. 'Am I dreaming,' he demanded unsteadily, 'or did you just tell me you love me?'

'Perhaps we're both dreaming,' whispered Ginny tremulously, the beautiful, fuzzy feeling stirring in her interfering with her enunciation. She slipped her hands beneath his sweater, letting them luxuriate against the satin warmth of his skin, while a happiness almost too much to bear swept aside the horrors that had possessed her for so long. 'But I do love you. I said the words a thousand times over in my heart each time we made love. . . And all those other times when I was still trying to deny it to myself.'

'Oh, Ginny,' he whispered with a shuddered sigh. 'I love you so much. I should have accepted loving you instead of screwing it all up by putting so much store on your telling me about Libby. How can I ever make up for the terrible things I've done to you?'

He crushed her to him as she made to protest, tenderness struggling to temper the hunger with which he kissed her. But it was he who broke away when her answering hunger threatened to engulf them both.

'Ginny, I need you—want you,' he whispered, hugging her fiercely to him. 'But I want to take you home to make love to you: back to the place I first found you—the place where we first made love. I want to take you back there and tell you all the things I should have told you but was too pig-headed to. Ginny, am I crazy—wanting, for the sake of our future, to exorcise the ghosts of the past from the place we both love?'

Ginny reached up and stroked her fingers against his cheek, as though testing to make sure he was real. 'I don't care if it's crazy,' she whispered huskily. 'It's exactly the way I feel.'

He gave a soft, growling chuckle, a sultry wickedness entering his eyes as his hands began exploring the contours of the body clinging in unconscious seduction to his.

'How soon can you be ready for us to leave for home?' he asked, lowering his head and nuzzling his mouth against hers. 'I'm already having this problem relating to will-power.'

'Perhaps if you did something about your hands, it would be less of a problem for us both,' Ginny suggested unsteadily, having to contend not only with the havoc those hands were wreaking on her, but also the giddy joy that attacked her each time he said home—as though it were a concept in which she was automatically included.

'My hands?' he exclaimed in mock indignation. 'Yours are part of the reason I'm having all these problems!'

Happiness bubbled over into laughter in her as she reluctantly removed her hands which, to her surprise, had somehow slipped themselves beneath his waistband and begun exploring, quite shamelessly, low against his back.

'Ginny, my darling, I'll wait forever, if that's what you want,' he whispered. 'But just how soon can I take you home?'

'You'd wait forever?' she teased contentedly.

'Hell, no—I was lying,' he groaned through laughter. 'I just don't want you treading on any toes here. . . Darling, I mean that. We'll tie up whatever needs tying up before we leave.'

'There's nothing here to tie up,' she murmured dreamily. 'Except my Premium Bond winnings—and I can always pay those into the bank in——'

'Your what?'

When she had finished explaining, he hugged her to him, laughing. 'Perhaps you shouldn't have told me,' he teased. 'You could spend the rest of your life wondering if I've married you for your money.' He tensed suddenly, then took her by the arms and held her from him, all laughter gone from the eyes burning down into hers. 'Am I assuming too much?' he asked hoarsely. '*Will* you marry me?'

'Yes, I'll marry you,' she exclaimed, hurling herself back into his arms. 'Even though I know it's only my winnings you're after!'

'But do you also know you're making me so happy

it's scaring the pants off me?' he whispered unsteadily. 'All those things I said and did. . . I was fighting against loving you all the while: horrifying myself by displaying sides to me I didn't even know existed. And all those things I didn't say—like explaining about that friend of Libby's I was supposed to have——'

'Hush—I love you. I don't need explanations,' whispered Ginny, silencing his distracted outburst. She wound her arms around his neck, the sweetness of the peace she had last known as a small child reviving in her soul as she wrapped him in the protection of her love. 'We were both fighting the same battle,' she whispered, 'and the only thing that matters is that we both lost.'

He drew back slightly from her clinging arms to gaze down at her from love-filled eyes. Then his expression began changing, its teasing seduction playing havoc with her already over-burdened senses. 'I guess you're right. And there's another battle we're certain to lose if one of us——' He broke off, his grin filled with wickedness and love as he tilted his head towards distant sounds. 'Thank God—we have company,' he laughed, as the murmur of voices drifted to them from the hall. He released her, taking one of her hands firmly in his and gazing down at her with teasing, loving contentment. 'I guess I forgot to tell you that, right this minute, Libby is probably putting the finishing touches to her plans for our wedding. . . So how about if we help her out by issuing our first invitation?'